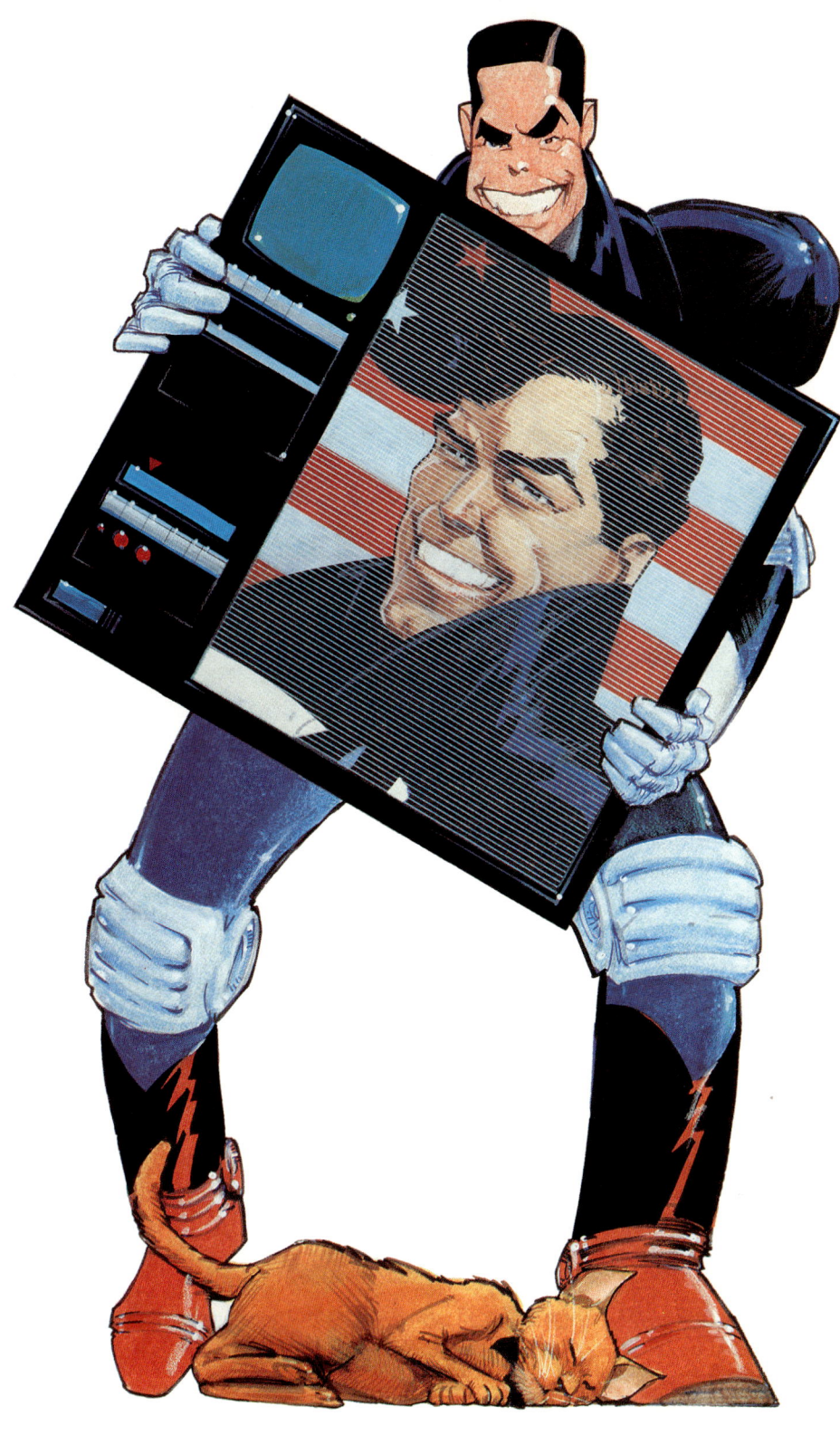

A/P

Howard Chaykin's

STATE of the UNION

HOWARD CHAYKIN
creator/writer/artist

LESLIE ZAHLER
colorist

KEN BRUZENAK
letterer

MIKE GOLD
editor

Dossiers by Charles Meyerson and Laurel Fitch

American Flagg!: State of the Union
Hardbound Edition

Bob Chapman, Publisher

We would like to thank the following people at First Publishing for their help and cooperation:

Rick Obadiah, Publisher

Kathy Kotsivas, Operations Director

Kurt Goldzung, Sales Director

Laurel Fitch, Editor

Alex Wald, Art Director

Mike McCormick, Production Manager

Rich Markow, Traffic Manager

American Flagg!: State of the Union (First Publishing Graphic Novel) ISBN: 0-915419-51-3 is published by First Publishing, Inc., 435 N. LaSalle, Chicago, IL 60610 and is copyright © 1989 First Publishing, Inc. and Howard Chaykin, Inc. The contents of American Flagg!: State of the Union (Limited Hardcover Edition Number 17) ISBN: 0-936211-15-6 are prepared under exclusive license from First Publishing, Inc. and published by Graphitti Designs, 1140 N. Kraemer Blvd., Unit B, Anaheim, CA 92806-1919 and is copyright © 1989 Graphitti Designs.

All rights reserved, including the right to reproduce this book or any portion thereof in any form whatsoever. The stories, incidents, and characters mentioned in this publication are entirely fictional. No actual persons, living or dead, without satiric content, are intended or should be inferred. Reuben Flagg and all prominent characters in this issue are trademarks of First Publishing, Inc. and Howard Chaykin, Inc.

Printed in the United States of America.
This edition is limited to 1800 printings.

After the food riots, banking collapse, earthquakes, and limited nuclear exchanges that plagued "The Year of the Domino," government and business fled Earth. But they needed to keep the remaining people happy. So they built... shopping malls. The Plexmalls, located in the major cities, provide jobs, homes, food, recreation, shelter from fallout, and defense.

As the absentee Plex's Earthside militia, the Rangers have the thankless task of maintaining "law and order." Their ranks are filled mostly by draft, although some — like Reuben Flagg — actually enlist out of loyalty. Rangers have a wide choice of exotic weaponry, including the Magrum .666™, Buzznucks™, and the Snowball 99™, used for crowd control.

The three stars represent Mars, Luna and Earth. It's also the symbol of the "Tricenntenial Recovery Committee," a Plex-inspired PR campaign ostensibly designed to get America *"Back on the track for '76!"*

THE HONORABLE CHARLES KEENAN BLITZ

Despite his respectable standing now, Mayor C.K. Blitz has a rather notorious past: co-founder with Hilton Krieger of the motorcycle club known as the Genetic Warlords.

Thirteen arrests later, the government realized he was perfect law enforcement material and made him one of the first "Plexus Rangers," giving C.K. the contacts and clout that led him to the mayor's office.

But Mayor Blitz hasn't wholeheartedly embraced law and order. On the side, he owns an illegal sports franchise, the Skokie Skullcrushers, a basketball team with a reputation for pounding their opponents — literally.

The Mayor also owns a pair of robotic bodyguards named Bert and Ernie — a joke that he maintains no one under 40 can understand.

MEDEA BLITZ!

When "Hammerhead" Krieger returned after a three-year hitch in Carracas, he found his wife, Peg, had had a second little girl — Medea — by C.K. Blitz. And Medea is Daddy's little girl: following in her father's footsteps, she served as treasurer of the Genetic Warlords.

Well known in Chicago as a "cycle slut," Medea was carrying Hilton Krieger's child and looking to collect big blackmail when he was murdered. For a time Medea and her boyfriend were the prime suspects until Reuben Flagg cleared them. Tranquilized into nirvana, Medea elected to join the Rangers and left for training in Brasilia.

Even though they're half-sisters, there's little love lost between Medea and Mandy Krieger.

Raul's a cat.

He *talks*. That doesn't seem to bother people much, but then maybe they're just being polite.

Raul was Hilton Krieger's cat. He trusted Raul more than any human he knew and left him the key to Q-USA. After Hilton was blown away, Raul followed orders and gave the key to Flagg. Raul now considers himself Reuben's cat.

Raul drinks White Russians and, like all cats, is a little egotistical. But that's never stopped him from demanding the use of any free hand for a quick scratch under the chin.

RAUL

WITNESSES

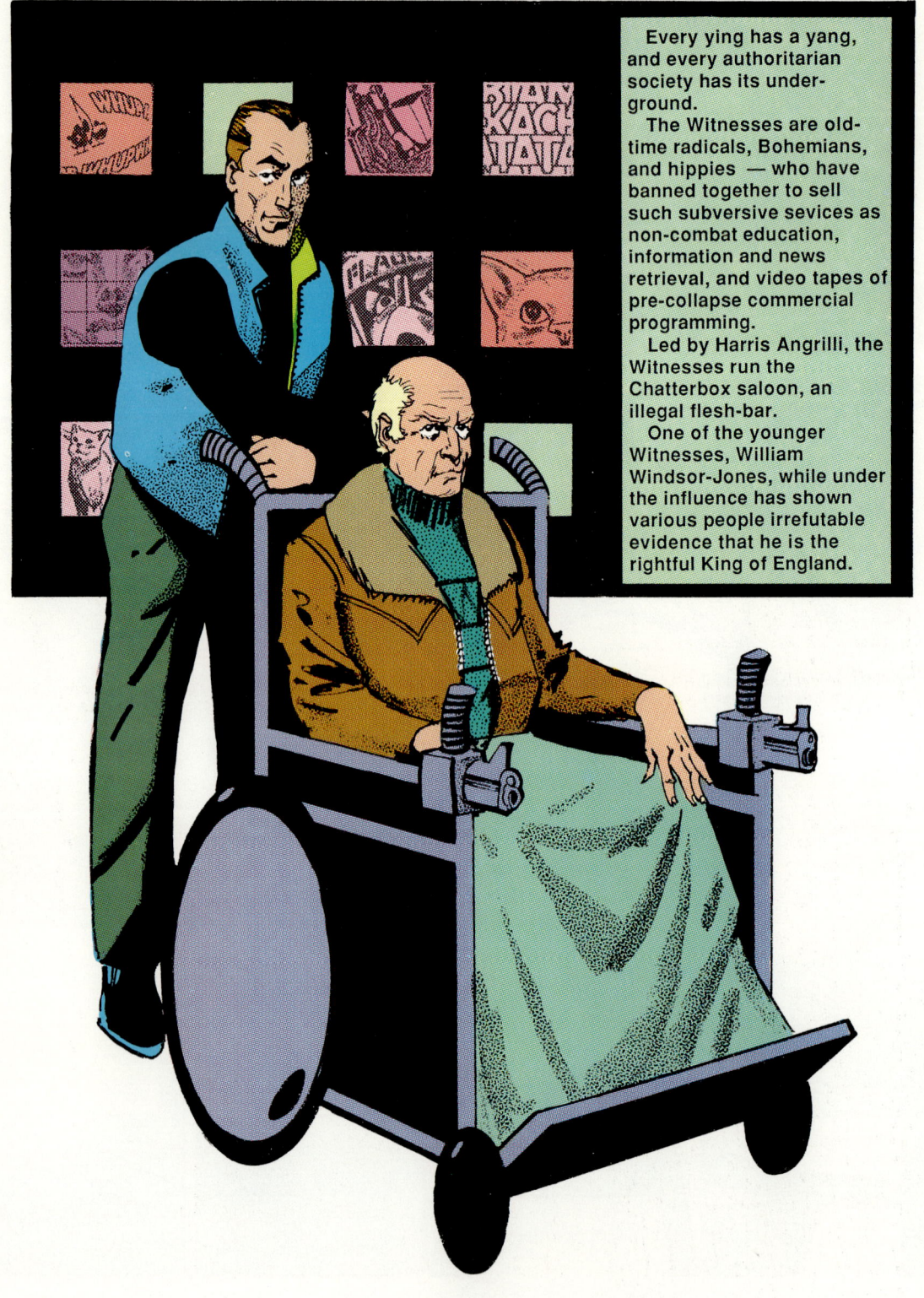

Every ying has a yang, and every authoritarian society has its underground.

The Witnesses are old-time radicals, Bohemians, and hippies — who have banned together to sell such subversive sevices as non-combat education, information and news retrieval, and video tapes of pre-collapse commercial programming.

Led by Harris Angrilli, the Witnesses run the Chatterbox saloon, an illegal flesh-bar.

One of the younger Witnesses, William Windsor-Jones, while under the influence has shown various people irrefutable evidence that he is the rightful King of England.

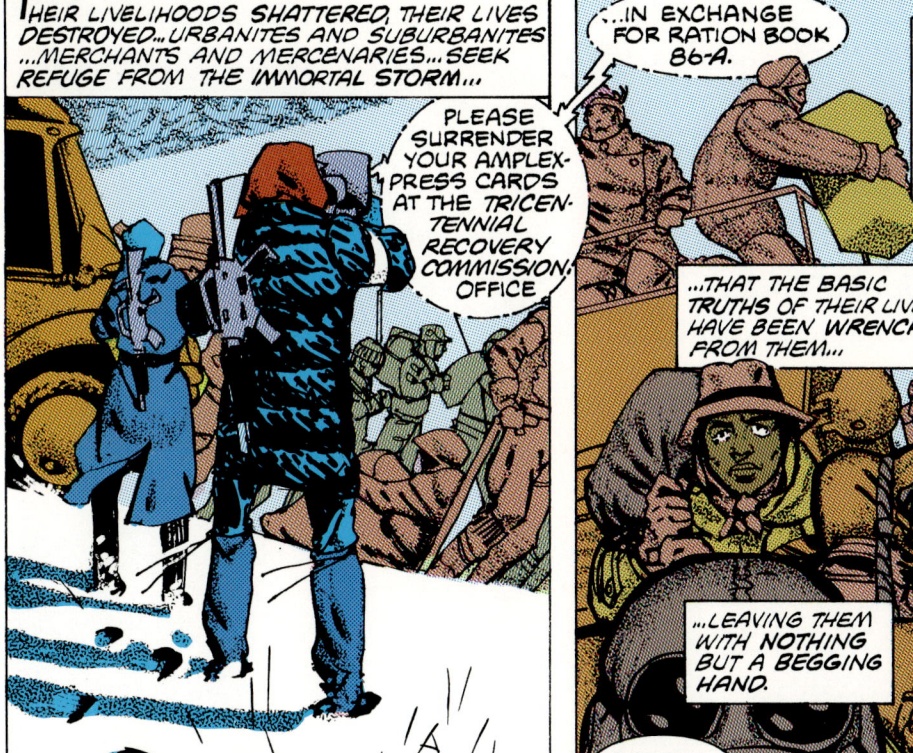

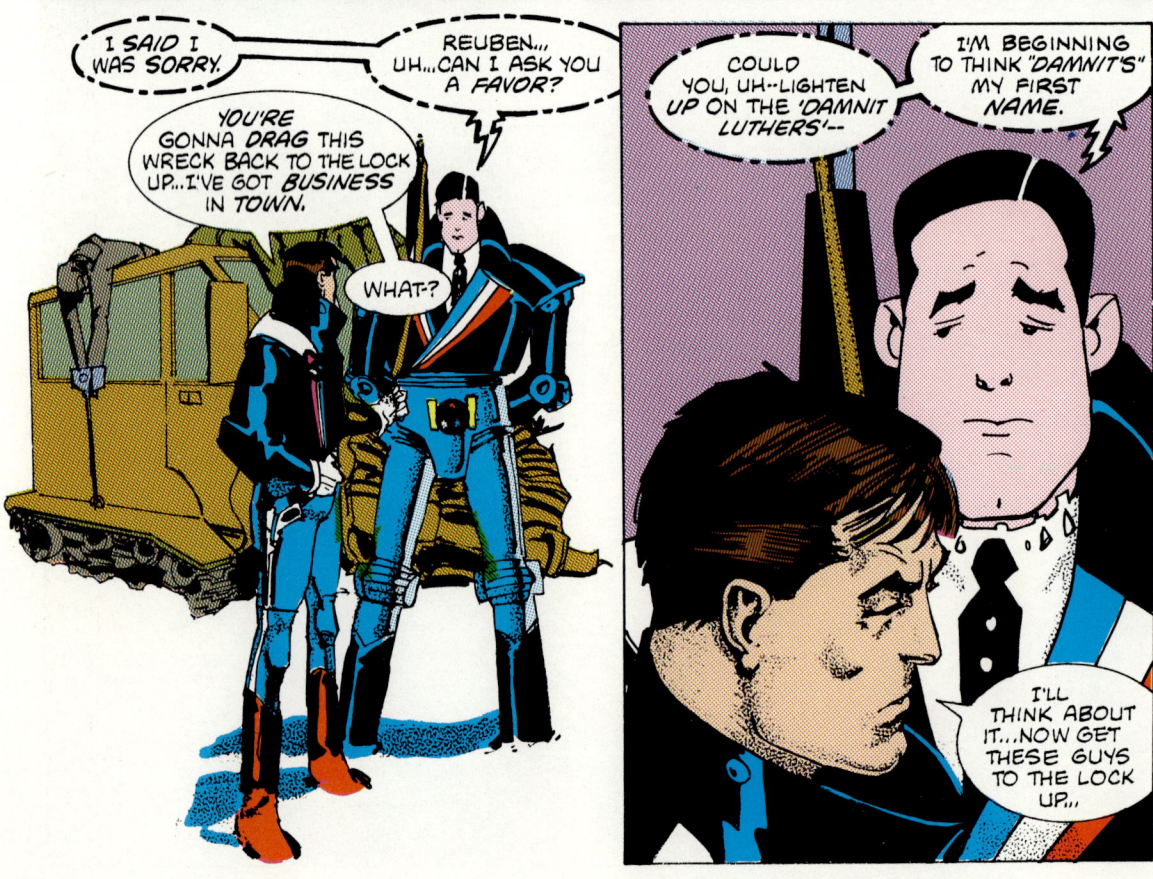

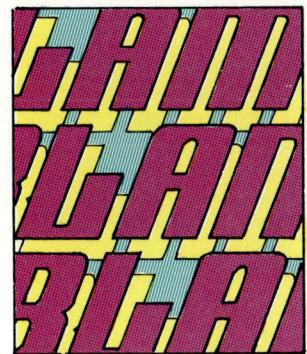

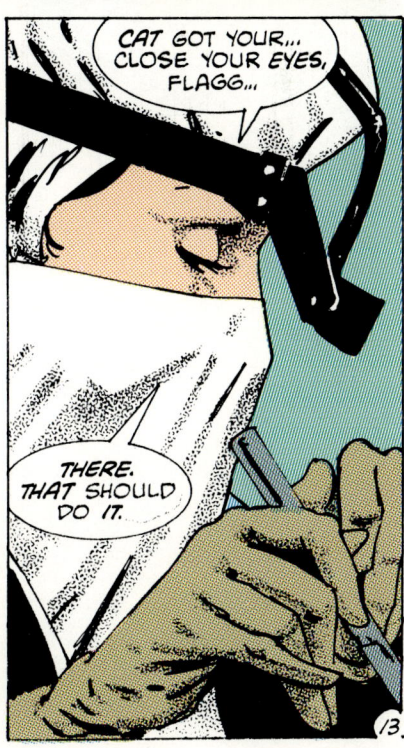

"DR. WEIS?"
"SPEAKING."
"MY NAME IS DECKER..."
"I'VE BEEN EXPECTING YOUR CALL."
KLIK

"I TRUST THE DESIGNS FOR THE DEVICE WE SUBCONTRACTED THROUGH YOUR SUPERIORS HAVE BEEN DELIVERED TO THE MALL?"
"DAY AFTER CHRISTMAS."
"I DON'T UNDERSTAND."
"ACCIDENT... A LIFE OR DEATH SITUATION ON THE HIGHWAY..."

"...I HAD TO PERFORM EMERGENCY SURGERY. I GAVE THE CASSETTE TO THE PLEXUS RANGER... HE PROMISED TO GET IT TO JERRY RIGG..."
"RANGER FLAGG...MY GOD..."
"HE SEEMED TRUSTWORTHY..."
"YEAH. (SNORT) HE'S A REAL BOY SCOUT..."

"LOOK, MR....DECKER, IS IT? I'VE JUST PERFORMED AN EXTREMELY COMPLEX OPERATION ON A LUNCH COUNTER..."
"...MY NERVES ARE RAW... AND MY SENSE OF HUMOR ISN'T QUITE UP TO PAR."

"I WAS TOLD BY MY SUPERIORS THAT YOU WOULD BRIEF ME..."

"OF COURSE. SORRY."
"I'M SURE YOU'RE AWARE OF THE MUTUAL NON-AGRESSION PACT SIGNED BY YOUR CADRE AND OTHER SIMILARLY ALIGNED CLUBS..."
"CERTAINLY. THE "AMERICA NOW" TREATY."
"WHAT YOU'RE NOT AWARE OF IS THE SOURCE OF THE PACT."
"DR. WEIS... ARE YOU FAMILIAR WITH AN ORGANIZATION CALLED THE AMERICAN SURVIVALIST LABOR COMMITTEE?"

THE CITY...

15

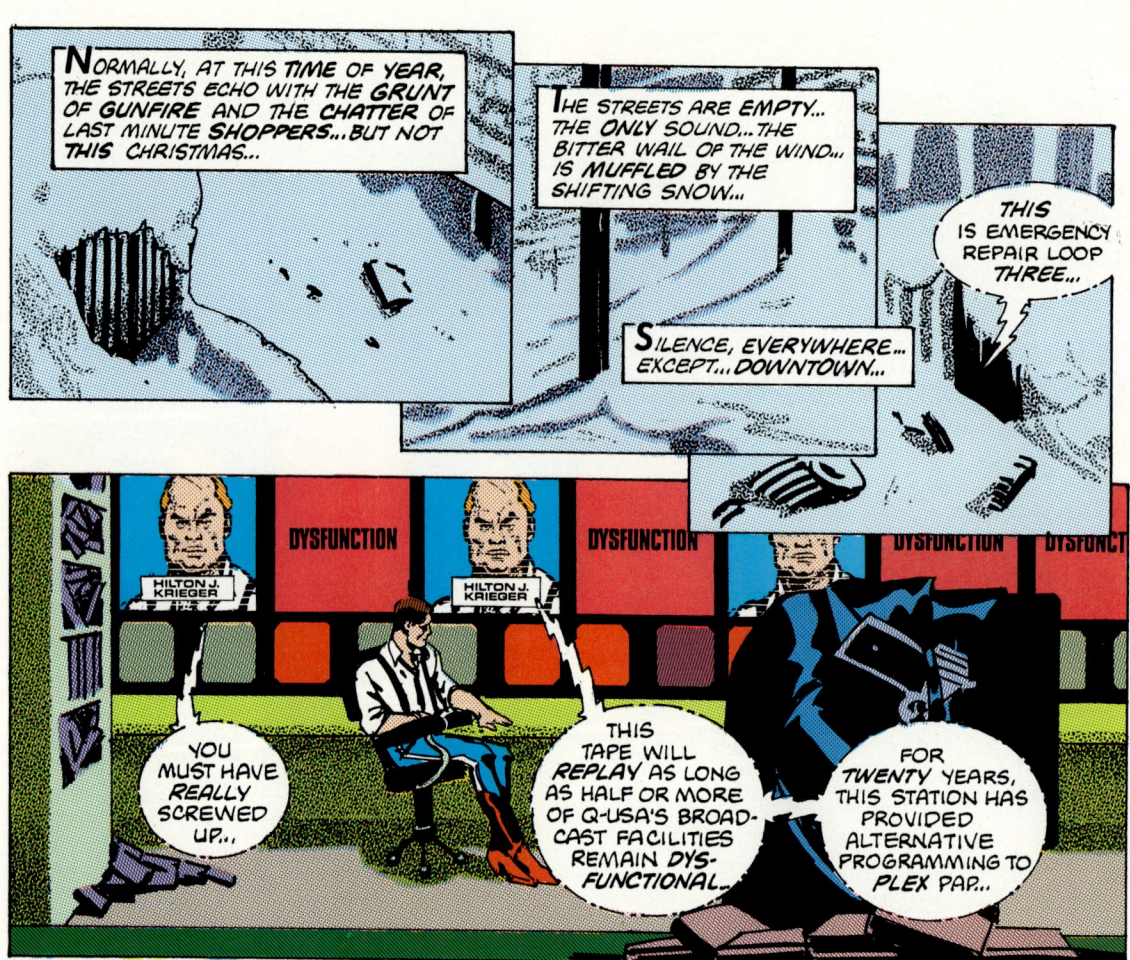

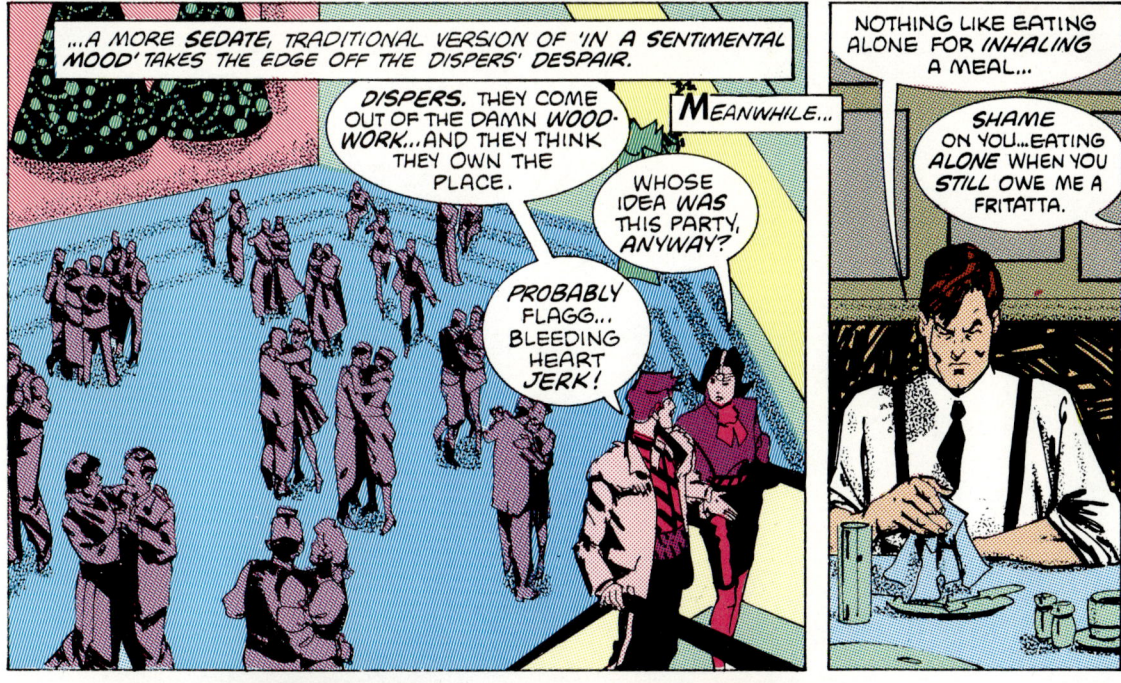

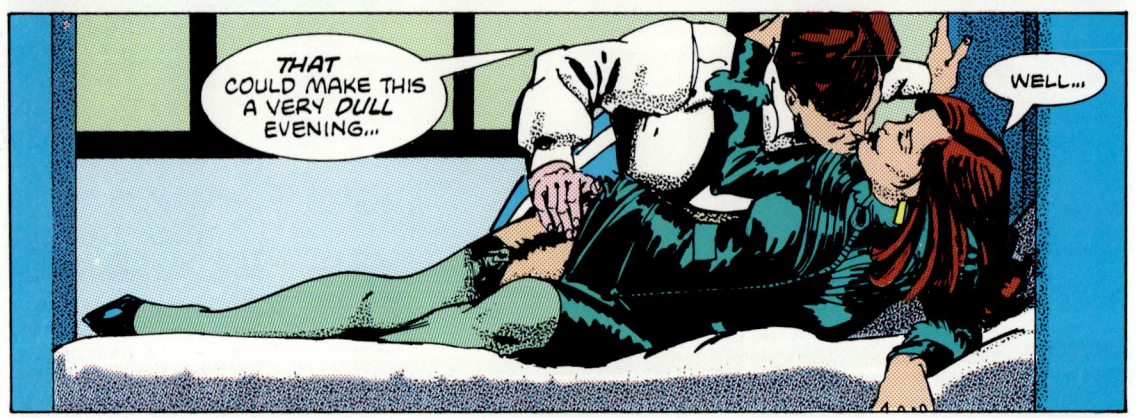

--IS THE PROBLEM?

A SWASTIKA?

WHAT DO YOU EXPECT FROM A MEDICAL OFFICER IN THE NORTH SIDE SS?

A NAZI!

NAZI? WHERE HAVE YOU BEEN? WE'RE THE GOTTER-DAMMERCRATS NOW.

A NAZI! I THOUGHT YOU WERE...

A NICE JEWISH DOCTOR, RIGHT?

MY GRANDFATHER WAS A JEW FOR JESUS BACK IN '75... THAT WAS THAT...

ANYWAY, WHY MIX POLITICS AND SEX?

BESIDES... ADMIT IT...

...DOESN'T IT GIVE THE SCENE...A CERTAIN EDGE...

THAT TURNS YOU ON...JUST A BIT?

OWW!

THAT'S ONE WAY TO DEAL WITH IT--!

ALL RIGHT! COME HERE LOVER...

23

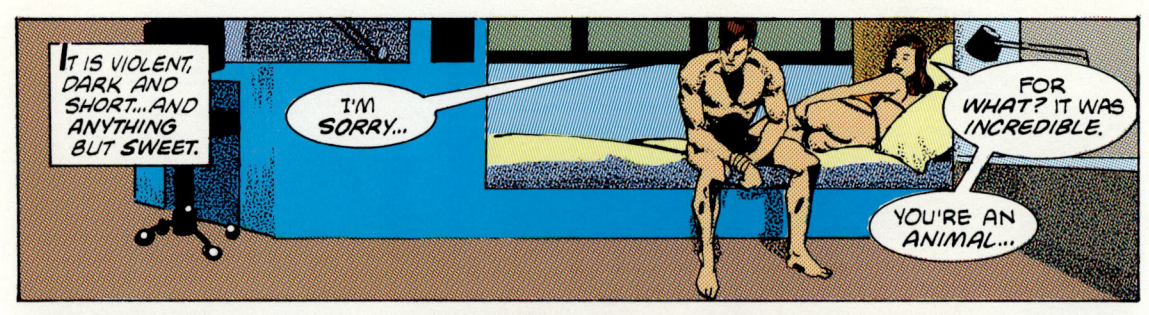

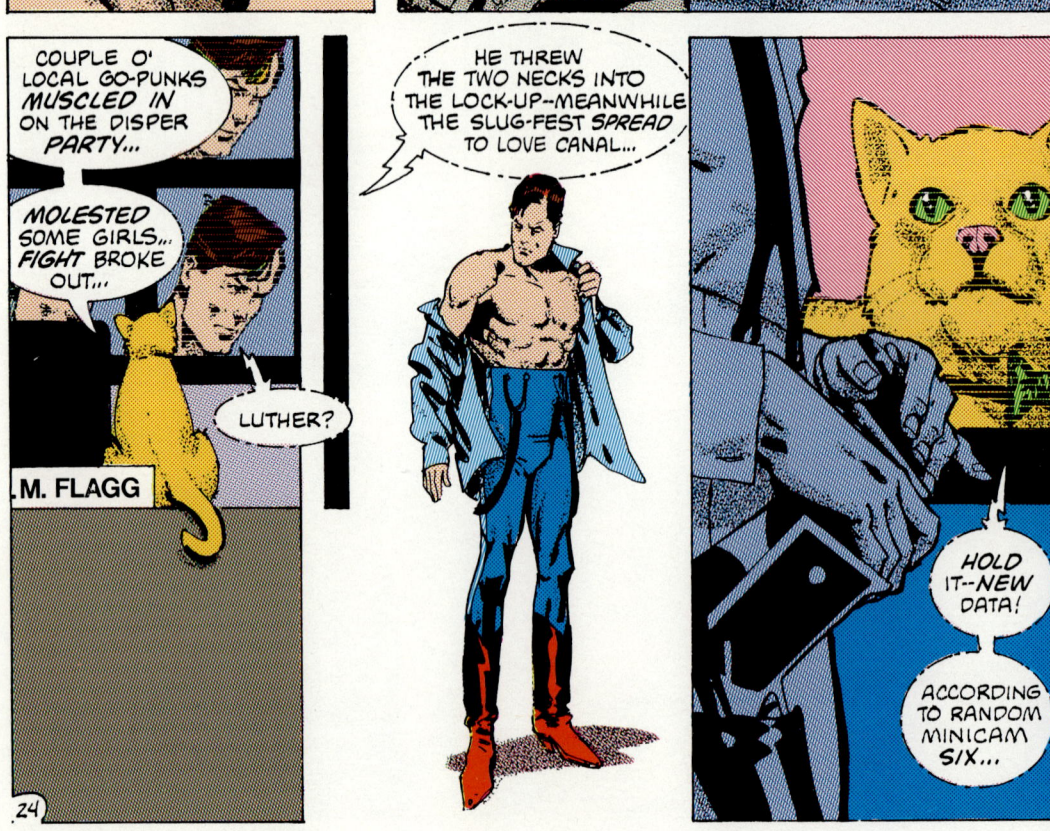

IT IS VIOLENT, DARK AND SHORT...AND ANYTHING BUT SWEET.

I'M SORRY...

FOR WHAT? IT WAS INCREDIBLE.

YOU'RE AN ANIMAL...

THAT WAS JUST ANGER, FIRED BY SELF-LOATHING...

C'MON-- I'LL TAKE YOU TO YOUR--

BZZZ

SORRY TO INTERRUPT REUBEN--BUT WE'VE GOT A PROBLEM...

WHAT?

COUPLE O' LOCAL GO-PUNKS MUSCLED IN ON THE DISPER PARTY...

MOLESTED SOME GIRLS... FIGHT BROKE OUT...

LUTHER?

HE THREW THE TWO NECKS INTO THE LOCK-UP--MEANWHILE THE SLUG-FEST SPREAD TO LOVE CANAL...

HOLD IT-- NEW DATA!

ACCORDING TO RANDOM MINICAM SIX....

M. FLAGG

"ONE OF THE DISPERS HAS A GUN!"

ONE MORE SHOT AND I'LL KILL HIM--I PROMISE!

DAMNIT, LUTHER-- HOLD YOUR FIRE--!

SORRY, MANDY--

HE'S GOT C.K.--!

EITHER YOU GIVE ME THE SCUM THAT RAPED MY DAUGHTER...

OR THE NIGGER DIES! I SWEAR TO GOD!

HOW'D THEY GET C.K. WITH BERT AND ERNIE GUARDING HIS BODY?

I--UH-- ACCIDENTALLY SHOT 'EM IN THE MELEE UPSTAIRS...

AND WHERE THE HELL IS REUBEN?

I'VE GOT TO DO THIS THE HARD WAY...

'CAUSE I'M TOO SHAKY FOR A CLEAN SHOT.
FOR GOD'S SAKE-- A SWASTIKA.
I DON'T REMEMBER EVER BEING THIS ASHAMED OF MYSELF..
I'M COUNTING TO TEN... ONE...
KLIK
BUZZZZZ
GET DOWN, C.K.!
UNGK!
BUZZZZZZ
RRRRRRRRRR
BOJEMOI!

RRIPPPPP!
SPLOSHH!
BUZZZZZZZZZZZZZZZZZ
HOLD YOUR-
-FIRE!
ZOTZ!
MOMENTS LATER...
YOU'RE SURE YOU'RE OKAY, C.K.?
JUST FINE--NO THANKS TO MY BODY-GUARDS.
CONSIDER-ING WHAT SHORT WORK HE MADE OF BERT AND ERNIE...
...MAYBE I SHOULD MAKE LUTHER MY BODYGUARD...
AND HAVE MEDEA ASSIGNED AS YOUR DEPUTY.

FLAGG?
HE'S OVER BY THE ELEVATORS...
THANKS.
MEDEA BLITZ AS MY DEPUTY... GIVE ME STRENGTH...
REUBEN--REUBEN, WAIT...!
CRYSTAL...?!
TITANIA--!
YOU GOTTA HELP ME WITH THIS--
HAVE YOU SEEN THE MAYOR?
MANDY JUST TOOK HIM DOWNSTAIRS TO MEET MEDEA ON THE BULLET.
SHE NEVER GOT ON THE TRAIN.
THAT FOOL SANTOS DECIDED TO BYPASS THE RAIL TERMINAL AND BRING THE BEL GEDDES IN HERE...
HE FLEW HER SQUARE INTO AN ICE STORM, BACKED BY 75 M.P.H. CROSSWINDS...
"THEY HAVEN'T RESPONDED ON ANY HAILING FREQUENCY FOR THREE HOURS...

WE'LL RETURN TO PUBLIC HUMILIATOR™ IN A MOMENT... BUT FIRST, THIS WORD FROM YOUR LOCAL PLEXUS RANGERS...
REUBEN...
WHAT?
CAN I DRIVE?
NO.
FRIENDS... IT'S NO SECRET THAT THE NEW MIDWEST HAS PROBLEMS ENOUGH... 70% UNEMPLOYMENT, CONSTANT INTERGANG WARFARE, AND MALAISE ON AN EPIC SCALE...
WITHOUT THE ADDITIONAL HEARTACHE OF THE WORST BLIZZARD IN CHICAGO'S HISTORY...
Plexus Ranger Reuben Flagg
WITH SOCIAL SERVICES AND PRIVATE ENTERPRISE DECIMATED BY NEARLY TWENTY FEET OF SNOW SINCE THANKSGIVING... (TWENTY FEET!)...
...THE PLEX, WITH YOUR LOCAL TRICENTENNIAL RECOVERY COMMISSION, HAS STEPPED IN TO OFFER SHELTER TO THE DISENFRANCHISED VICTIMS OF THE STORM.
RIGHT, REUBEN. SURE... IT'S BEEN A MASSIVE DRAG FOR THE MALL, PROVIDING FOOD AND EMERGENCY SHELTER FOR THE DISPERS...
BUT, REALLY, DOES ANYONE AT KRIEGER PLEXMALL WANT TO BE THE FIRST TO SAY... "NO ROOM AT THE INN?"
YOU BET, RAUL. AND, AS FOR THE SKYROCKETING CRIME RATE... IT SHOULD BE NOTED...
THAT THE LARGEST PERCENTAGE OF THE INCREASE IS IN CRIME COMMITTED AGAINST THE MIGRANTS BY LOCAL GO-PUNKS.

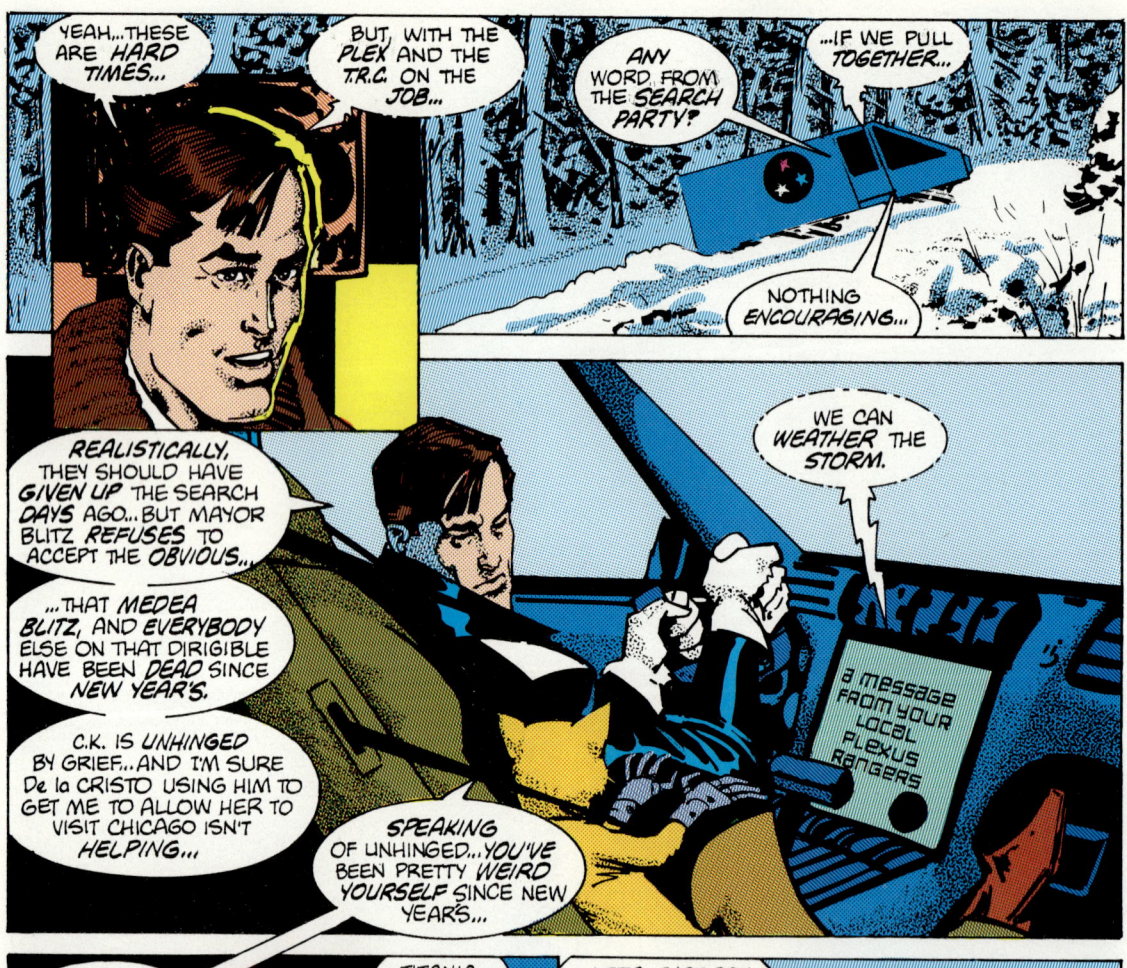

"YEAH...THESE ARE *HARD TIMES*..." "BUT, WITH THE *PLEX* AND THE *T.R.C.* ON THE *JOB*..." "ANY WORD FROM THE *SEARCH PARTY*?" "...IF WE PULL *TOGETHER*..."

"NOTHING *ENCOURAGING*..."

"*REALISTICALLY*, THEY SHOULD HAVE *GIVEN UP* THE SEARCH *DAYS AGO*...BUT MAYOR BLITZ *REFUSES* TO ACCEPT THE *OBVIOUS*..."

"...THAT *MEDEA BLITZ*, AND EVERYBODY ELSE ON THAT DIRIGIBLE HAVE BEEN *DEAD* SINCE *NEW YEAR'S*."

"*C.K.* IS *UNHINGED* BY GRIEF...AND I'M SURE DE LA CRISTO USING HIM TO GET ME TO ALLOW HER TO VISIT CHICAGO ISN'T *HELPING*..."

"WE CAN *WEATHER* THE STORM."

A MESSAGE FROM YOUR LOCAL PLEXUS RANGERS

"*SPEAKING* OF UNHINGED...YOU'VE BEEN PRETTY *WEIRD YOURSELF* SINCE NEW YEAR'S..."

"...ANYTHING TO DO WITH THAT *BIG CHICK* IN YOUR ROOM?"

"TITANIA *WEIS*?"

"LET'S JUST SAY I'M NOT USED TO FINDING *NATIONAL SOCIALISTS* IN MY BED AND LEAVE IT AT THAT..."

WAZZ

"THEY MUST BE *UNDERHANDED*...MOST OF THE FARM MILITIA'S OUT WITH HENRY ON THE *"BEL GEDDES"* SEARCH..."

"SOUNDS LIKE *A.S.L.C.*..."

ANIMAL MUTILATION IN PROGRESS
subdiv. no. six-
Rancho Deluxe

"COULD BE..."

2

RANCHO DELUXE
Div. SHAF'S
-Atomic Rooster Ltd.
A Plex Co.
Home of Mabel the Mutant Cow
MOOO MOOOO HONGK
YECCHH! I GOT BLOOD ON MY PANTS!
HONGK MOO HONGK
WHAT A WIMP!
SPANGK! BLAM! PONGK!
THROW DOWN YOUR GUNS AND PUT YOUR HANDS UP!
SOONER YOU GET THAT BACK END SEPARATED...
..SOONER WE CAN HAUL ASS OUT OF HERE!
MOO MOOO MOOO MOOO MOO
BLAM!
HONGKLE!
BLAM!
PUT DOWN YOUR GUNS--
DAMNIT FOXY--LOOK WHERE YOU SHOOT--
--YA KILLED ANOTHER COW!
WHAT IN HELL WAS THAT?

STATE OF
KATAWHUMPH
THAT WAS YOUR GET AWAY CAR...
...GETTING SOME MUCH NEEDED BODY WORK!
CHA-PUNT! *
KRANKLE
brought to you by
writer/artist:HOWARD CHAYKIN
letterer:KEN BRUZENAK
colorist:LESLIE ZAHLER
editor:MIKE GOLD
* RUBBER BULLETS, OF COURSE.
4

THE UNION PART 2
I'LL GET 'IM, FOXY--
GODDAMN HOTSHOT RANGERS--
--Y'D THINK THEY NEVER LEARN TO USE A--
DOOOOOO
THUD!
URNGNK!
RRRRR
REUBEN--! DUCK!
HOLY SH--
WHAT ARE YOU--
--CRAZY?!?
TRYING TO KILL ME--
5.

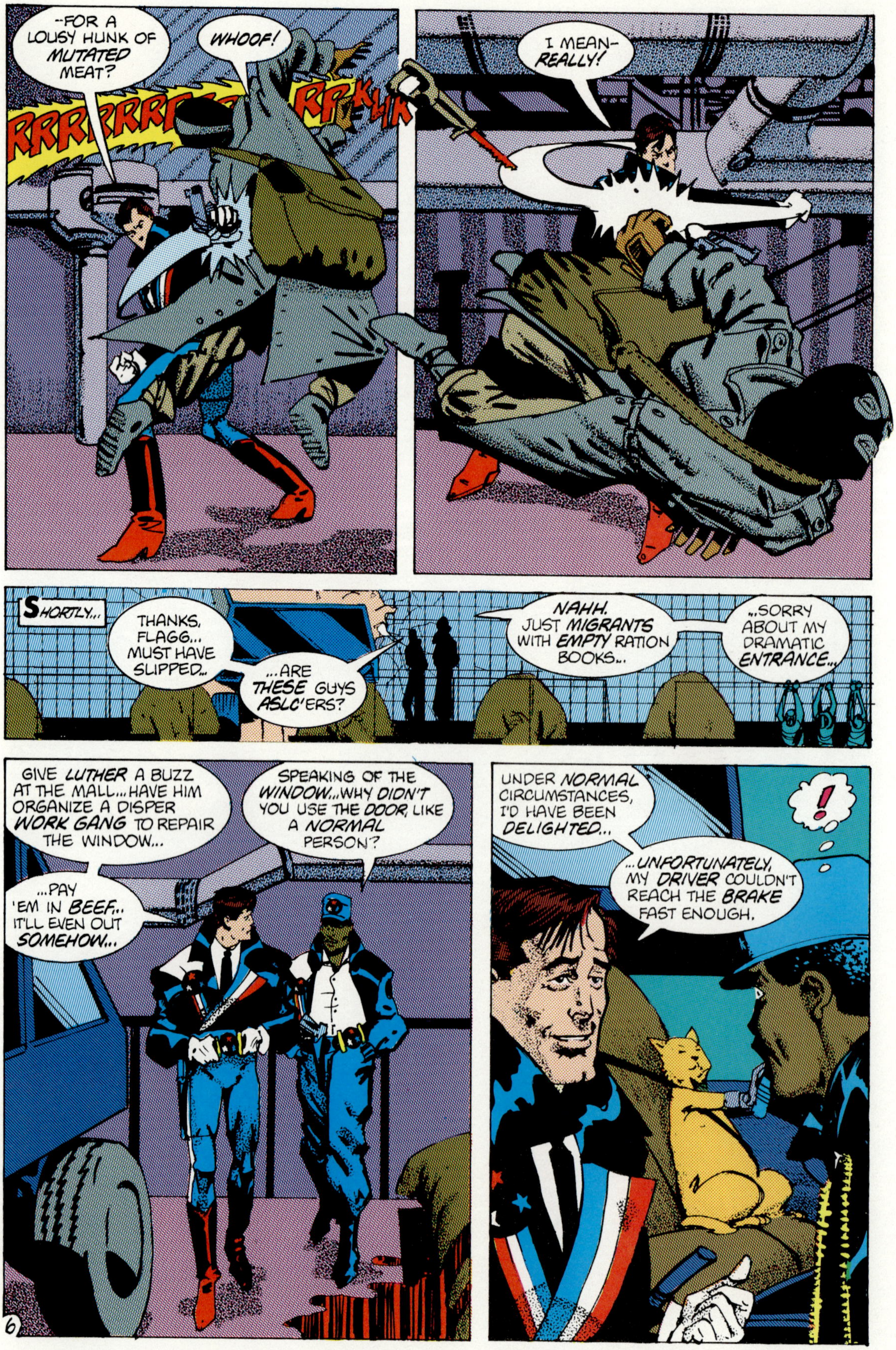

--FOR A LOUSY HUNK OF MUTATED MEAT?
WHOOF!
RRRRRRRRR
RRRKLIK
I MEAN-- REALLY!
SHORTLY...
THANKS, FLAGG... MUST HAVE SLIPPED...
...ARE THESE GUYS ASLC'ERS?
NAHH. JUST MIGRANTS WITH EMPTY RATION BOOKS...
...SORRY ABOUT MY DRAMATIC ENTRANCE...
GIVE LUTHER A BUZZ AT THE MALL... HAVE HIM ORGANIZE A DISPER WORK GANG TO REPAIR THE WINDOW...
...PAY 'EM IN BEEF.. IT'LL EVEN OUT SOMEHOW...
SPEAKING OF THE WINDOW... WHY DIDN'T YOU USE THE DOOR, LIKE A NORMAL PERSON?
UNDER NORMAL CIRCUMSTANCES, I'D HAVE BEEN DELIGHTED...
...UNFORTUNATELY, MY DRIVER COULDN'T REACH THE BRAKE FAST ENOUGH.
!

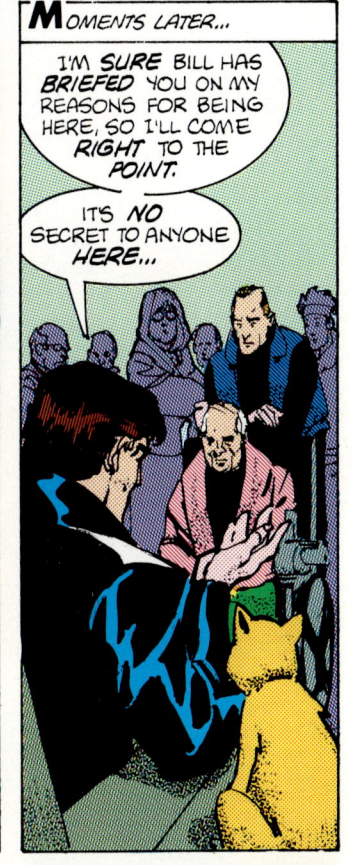

With no further detour, the BATTLEVAN™ roars downtown to the snowbound LOOP, where...

"You STILL haven't told me who these 'WITNESSES' are, or WHY we're--"

"SOON."

"HEY, BILL--HARRIS. YOU'RE LOOKING WELL."

"HELLO, REUBEN."

"GOOD TO SEE YOU, FLAGG--"

"WE'RE MEETING IN THE COMMON, WHEN YOU'RE READY, REUBEN..."

"AND THIS MUST BE RAUL."

"HEY, OLD GUY, HOW 'BOUT A RIDE?"

"RAUL!"

Moments later...

"I'M SURE BILL HAS BRIEFED YOU ON MY REASONS FOR BEING HERE, SO I'LL COME RIGHT TO THE POINT."

"IT'S NO SECRET TO ANYONE HERE..."

"...THAT WHEN HAMMERHEAD KRIEGER DIED, I INHERITED--RELUCTANTLY, I MIGHT ADD--THE PIRATE VIDEO STATION HE RAN FOR YEARS."

"I'D LOVE TO BLAME IT ON THE WEATHER...OR MY TRIP TO BRAZIL..."

"BUT I'M JUST NOT CUT OUT FOR MOONLIGHTING AS A BUCCANEER BROADCASTER."

"REUBEN-- WHAT ARE YOU--"

"SORRY RAUL--THIS HAS TO BE--"

"FRANKLY, I'M DOING A LOUSY JOB."

"REUBEN--!"

"HUSH-- RAUL--"

"WHAT ARE YOU SUGGESTING?"

"WELL, HARRIS..."

7

I'M PROPOSING A MERGER...
...OF THE WITNESSES DATA GATHERING SERVICES...
...WITH THE BROADCAST FACILITIES OF Q-USA.
REUBEN-- ARE YOU NUTS? KRIEGER--
KRIEGER IS DEAD.
I'M Q-USA NOW...
AND I CAN'T RUN IT ALONE. DEALING WITH LIFE'S DAY TO DAY MORASS OF CRAP IS MORE THAN I CAN HANDLE AS IT IS...
I DON'T WANT TO HEAR ANY MORE ON THE SUBJECT...
NOT ANOTHER WORD.
BUT-
SOUNDS GOOD, REUBEN. I'LL HAVE OUR LEGAL DEPARTMENT DRAW UP THE NECESSARY PAPERS...
SHORTLY...
RAUL'S JUST OVERLY SENTIMENTAL, REUBEN... YOU MADE THE RIGHT DECISION.
HOPE SO, BILL. I GAVE YOU THE KEYS TO THE STATION?
YEAH. I'LL GET A COUPLE OF THE YOUNGER GUYS TO HELP ME PACK AND CART IT BACK HERE.
THANKS AGAIN, REUBEN. YOU WON'T REGRET IT.
TRUST ME RAUL...IT'S FOR THE BEST...
NO ONE EVER ASKED ME IF I WANTED TO BE A VIDEO FREEBOOTER...RAUL?
RAUL?!?
YE GODS--THIS IS THE END--!
NOW I'M GETTING THE SILENT TREATMENT...
...FROM A TALKING CAT.
8

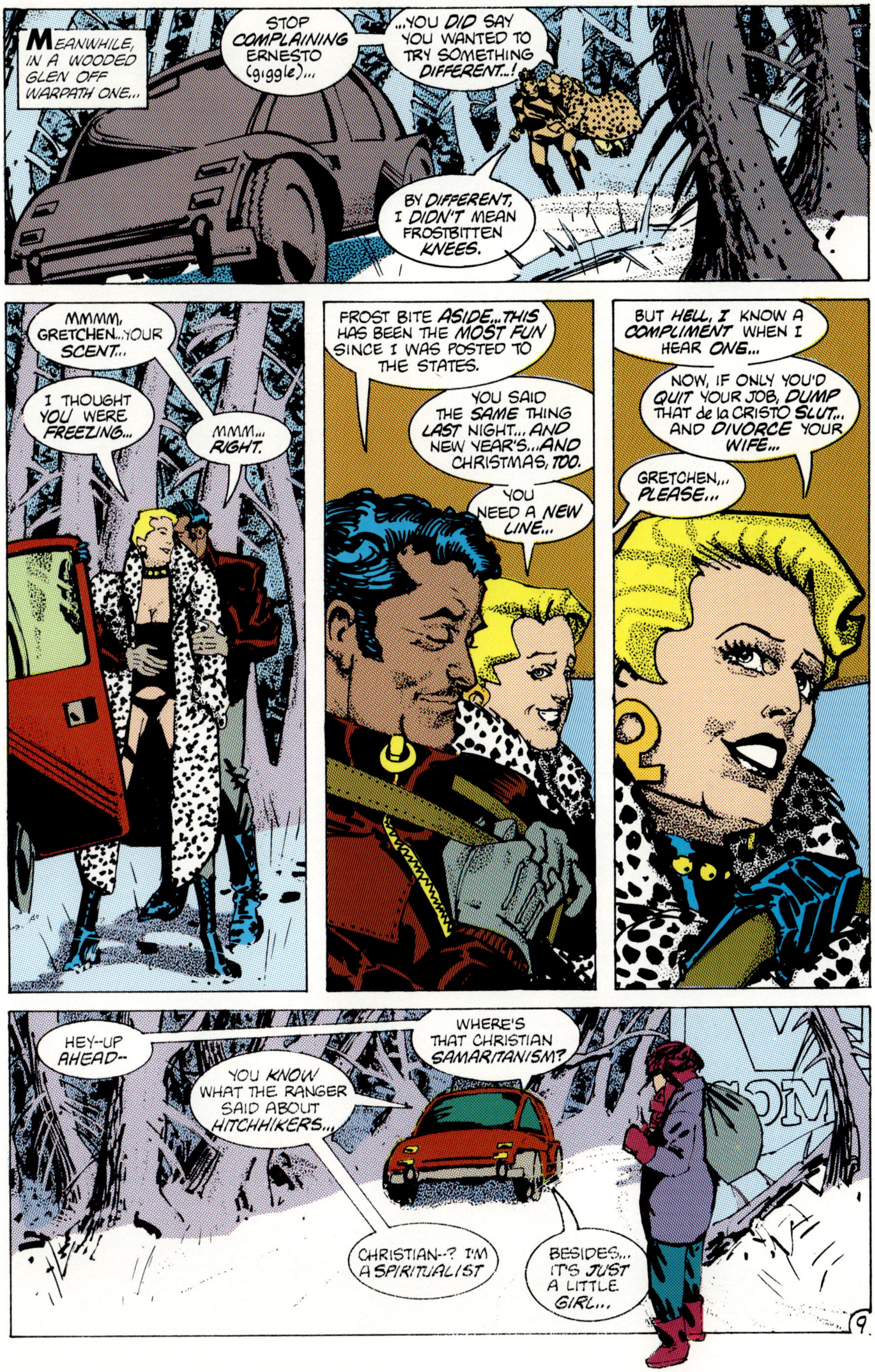
MEANWHILE, IN A WOODED GLEN OFF WARPATH ONE...
STOP COMPLAINING ERNESTO (giggle)...
...YOU DID SAY YOU WANTED TO TRY SOMETHING DIFFERENT...!
BY DIFFERENT, I DIDN'T MEAN FROSTBITTEN KNEES.
MMMM, GRETCHEN...YOUR SCENT...
I THOUGHT YOU WERE FREEZING...
MMM... RIGHT.
FROST BITE ASIDE...THIS HAS BEEN THE MOST FUN SINCE I WAS POSTED TO THE STATES.
YOU SAID THE SAME THING LAST NIGHT... AND NEW YEAR'S...AND CHRISTMAS, TOO.
YOU NEED A NEW LINE...
BUT HELL, I KNOW A COMPLIMENT WHEN I HEAR ONE...
NOW, IF ONLY YOU'D QUIT YOUR JOB, DUMP THAT de la CRISTO SLUT... AND DIVORCE YOUR WIFE...
GRETCHEN,,, PLEASE...
HEY--UP AHEAD--
WHERE'S THAT CHRISTIAN SAMARITANISM?
YOU KNOW WHAT THE RANGER SAID ABOUT HITCHHIKERS...
CHRISTIAN--? I'M A SPIRITUALIST
BESIDES... IT'S JUST A LITTLE GIRL...
9

FLAGG--WHAT THE HELL ARE YOU DOING HERE?
AFTER-NOON, YOUR HONOR...MS. de la CRISTO...
WHERE THE HELL SHOULD I BE?
WHY AREN'T YOU OUT SEARCH-ING FOR MEDEA WITH--
LOOK, C.K. I SYMPATHIZE WITH YOUR GRIEF...BUT I'VE GOT A JOB TO DO...
YOUR JOB IS TO FIND MY DAUGHTER.
LIKE HELL. MS. de la CRISTO HERE CALLED IN THE COMPANY'S SEARCH PARTY DAY BEFORE YESTERDAY...
...IF NOT FOR YOUR COMPLETE ABUSE OF OFFICE, HENRY WOULD'VE BROUGHT THE MILITIA HOME, TOO...
...MAYBE IT'S TIME YOU FACED REALITY...
RUDE, COLD-BLOODED BASTARD...
...YOU NEVER TOLD ME YOU CALLED OFF YOUR SEARCH PARTY, ESTER...
WELL...
HI, HENRY-- NO, IT'S LUTHER... REUBEN'S NOT...
WAIT A MINUTE-- HERE HE IS--
IT'S HENRY CHUNG--THEY FOUND THE ZEP--
GIVE IT HERE--
HEY, RAUL--WHAT COOKS?
RAUL--?

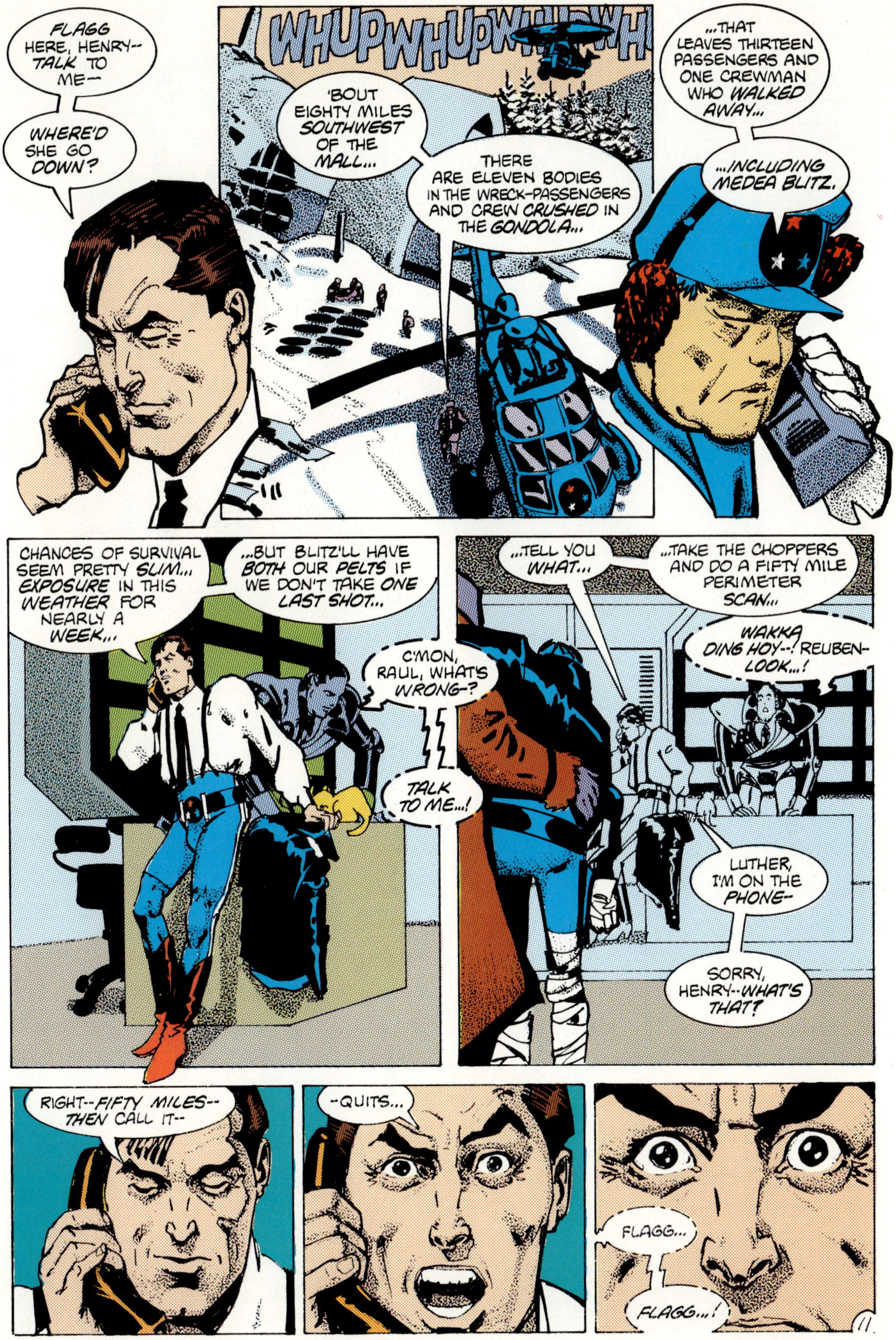
FLAGG HERE, HENRY-- TALK TO ME--
WHERE'D SHE GO DOWN?
WHUPWHUPWH
'BOUT EIGHTY MILES SOUTHWEST OF THE MALL...
THERE ARE ELEVEN BODIES IN THE WRECK-PASSENGERS AND CREW CRUSHED IN THE GONDOLA...
...THAT LEAVES THIRTEEN PASSENGERS AND ONE CREWMAN WHO WALKED AWAY...
...INCLUDING MEDEA BLITZ.
CHANCES OF SURVIVAL SEEM PRETTY SLIM... EXPOSURE IN THIS WEATHER FOR NEARLY A WEEK...
...BUT BLITZ'LL HAVE BOTH OUR PELTS IF WE DON'T TAKE ONE LAST SHOT...
C'MON, RAUL, WHAT'S WRONG--?
TALK TO ME...!
...TELL YOU WHAT...
...TAKE THE CHOPPERS AND DO A FIFTY MILE PERIMETER SCAN...
WAKKA DING HOY--! REUBEN-- LOOK...!
LUTHER, I'M ON THE PHONE--
SORRY, HENRY--WHAT'S THAT?
RIGHT--FIFTY MILES-- THEN CALL IT--
--QUITS...
FLAGG...
FLAGG...!

Panel 1:
"PLEXUS RANGER MEDEA...BLITZ... REPORTING FOR—"
"DUUUUTY..."
"FLAGG-- ARE YOU THERE?"

Panel 2:
"UH--HELLO, TITANIA... I...UH..."
"FLAGG-- WHAT'S GOING ON?"
"ZZZZZZ"
"THE OTHERS ARE IN THE MEDIPLEX...SHE INSISTED-- AT GUNPOINT-- THAT I BRING HER HERE..."

Panel 3:
"RAVING ABOUT SOMETHING TO PROVE."
"WHEN SHE COMES TO, YOU CAN TELL HER I DON'T LIKE WEAPONS SHOVED IN MY FACE...LEAST OF ALL BY MISCEGENATED HALF BREED MONGRELS. GOODBYE."
"UH...I..."
"FLAGG--!"
"ZZZZZZZZ"

Panel 4:
"FLAGG-- WHAT?"
"REUBEN?"
"TELL HIM TO BRING IN THE SEARCH DETAIL...I'LL CALL HIM BACK LATER..."

BRATATATAT
OPERATOR-- I'M TRYING TO REACH THE RANGERS...
CHUNT CHUNT
...WE'RE TRAVELLING IN A FREE ZONE...
BRATATAT
CHUNT CHUNT
I KNOW THE LINES ARE BUSY... THIS IS AN EMERGENCY...
AND THE CAR'S GOT TURF VISA PLATES ANYWAY--
...THEN WHO ARE THESE PEOPLE... AND WHY ARE THEY SHOOTING AT US?!?
CAN'T YOU--OH FORGET IT BUTTHEAD...
I'LL USE THE BEACON.
KLIK
THAT'S IT FOR THE AMMUNITION, GRETCHEN...
ANY SUGGESTIONS?
WITH YOUR DIPLOMATIC CREDENTIALS, MAYBE WE CAN WORK OUT A RANSOM...
THEY MUST BE FREEWAY-MEN...
NUH-UH-- THEY'RE NOT CROOKS...
KAR-WHAM
IT'S MY DAD.
SKLUSSH

DR. ROBERT... DR. PEPPER... DR. HOWARD... DR. FINE... DR. HOWARD...
NO DRUGS... NO ACCELLERANTS, NO STEROIDS...
REALLY..! THAT'S REMARKABLE...
REALLY... EXCEPT FOR SOME CUTS AND BRUISES FROM THE CRASH...
...AND THE EXPECTED EXHAUSTION AND... WELL, PAIN OF EXPOSURE...
...MEDEA IS IN SPECTACULAR SHAPE...
...AND SHE ASKED FOR YOU.
THANK YOU, DR. KRONKHEIT...
WELL, HELLO...
HOT DAMN--REAL CHOCOLATE! THANKS CRYSTAL...MANDY... HONESTLY.
OH, REUBEN...
AHEM...
I'M SORRY, REUBEN...I--
DON'T BE A SCHMUCK, C.K. YOU WERE BENT OUT OF SHAPE.
I DON'T MEAN TO BE RUDE, BUT FOR PROFESSIONAL ...AND PERSONAL REASONS...
I'D LIKE TO TALK TO REUBEN...
ALONE.
?!?
14

PLEASE... HAVE SOME CHOCOLATES... I CAN'T--

I'M A NEWLY DIAGNOSED DIABETIC...WHICH PARTIALLY ACCOUNTS FOR SOME OF MY MORE OFF THE WALL ANTICS IN THE PAST...

ONLY PARTIALLY... BUT BELIEVE ME WHEN I SAY...

...I'M NOT THE MEDEA YOU USED TO KNOW.

THIS BECOMES CLEARER BY THE MOMENT...

...WHAT HAPPENED?

WHEN THE "BEL GEDDES" FINALLY CAME TO A STOP...

...WE PULLED OURSELVES TOGETHER...PICKED OURSELVES UP....

...THE OFFICERS WERE DEAD... I JUST NATURALLY ASSUMED COMMAND...IT WAS WEIRD.

I GOT 'EM IN LINE... SLOWEST IN FRONT TO SET THE PACE... SINGLE FILE...

...WE MUST HAVE WALKED IN CIRCLES FOR DAYS 'TIL WE FOUND THE ROAD...BY ACCIDENT...

...WAS HOURS BEFORE WE SAW A CAR...

SHE WAS HALFWAY DOWN THE LINE WHEN IT FINALLY REGISTERED...SHE HAD NO INTENTION OF STOPPING.

SHE CAME RIGHT AT ME...

I FLASHED HER MY SHIELD...

BUT I THINK IT WAS MY AUTOMATIC THAT STOPPED HER.

15.

16

SHUT UP, YOU STUPID BITCH...!
WE'LL DO WHATEVER WE WANT WITH YOU...
...WHETHER WE KILL YOUR SPICK BOYFRIEND OR NOT...
...IT'D BE SECONDS FOR ALL OF US, ANYHOW! HAW!
AMY...? NAAH, I THREW A SECONAL IN HER OJ...
KEEP IT DOWN GEORGE...YOU'LL WAKE YOUR DAUGHTER.
...SHE'LL BE OUT COLD FOR A WHILE...
...'N SHE'S GONNA WAKE UP TO THE BEATING OF HER LIFE.
I STILL THINK WE SHOULD TAKE BLONDIE HERE...
...KEEP HER CHAINED UP IN ONE OF THE CAVES IN THE BACK-WOOD...
'N HOSE 'ER DOWN ON WEEKENDS FOR STAG PARTIES.
AS LONG AS HER LOOKS HOLD UP...
HAW-- BE FUN-- LONG'S MY WIFE DON'T KNOW...
PLEASE DON'T HIT HIM...
I TELL YOU BOYS... THIS TRAMP'S GOT A REAL WARM SPOT FOR THE JUNGLE STUD HERE...
'N SINCE HE'S NOT COMIN' WITH US...
...WE OUGHT TO BRING ALONG SOMETHIN' FOR HER TO REMEMBER HIM BY...
NO-- AAAAA-- NO!

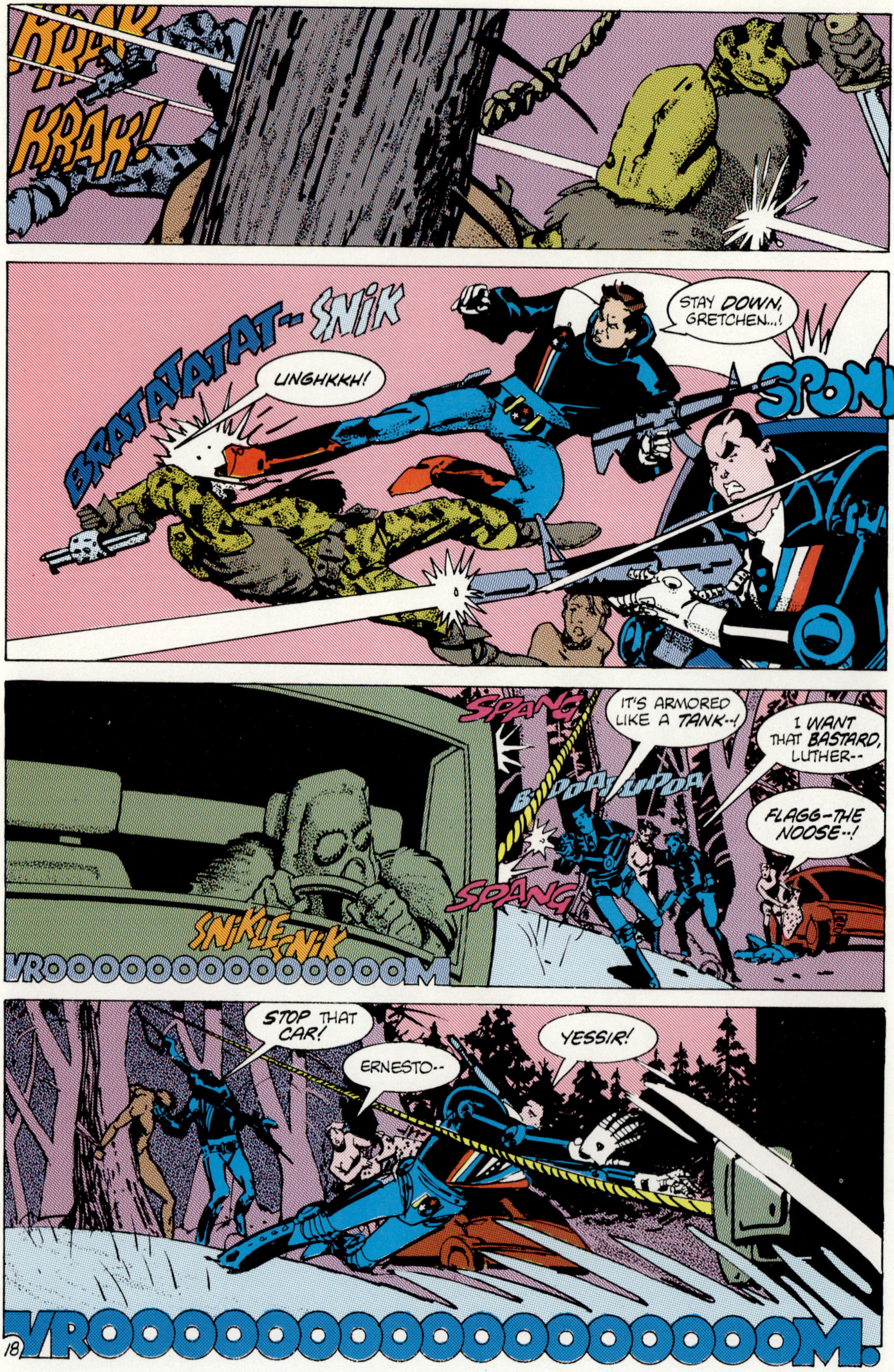
KRAK
KRAK!
BRATATATAT-- SNIK
STAY DOWN, GRETCHEN...!
UNGHKKH!
SPONK
SPANG
IT'S ARMORED LIKE A TANK--!
I WANT THAT BASTARD, LUTHER--
FLAGG--THE NOOSE--!
SPANG
SNIKLE-SNIK
VROOOOOOOOOOOOOOOM
STOP THAT CAR!
ERNESTO--
YESSIR!
VROOOOOOOOOOOOOOOOOOOOM!

SPLONGKSH!
PO'NCK! VROOOM

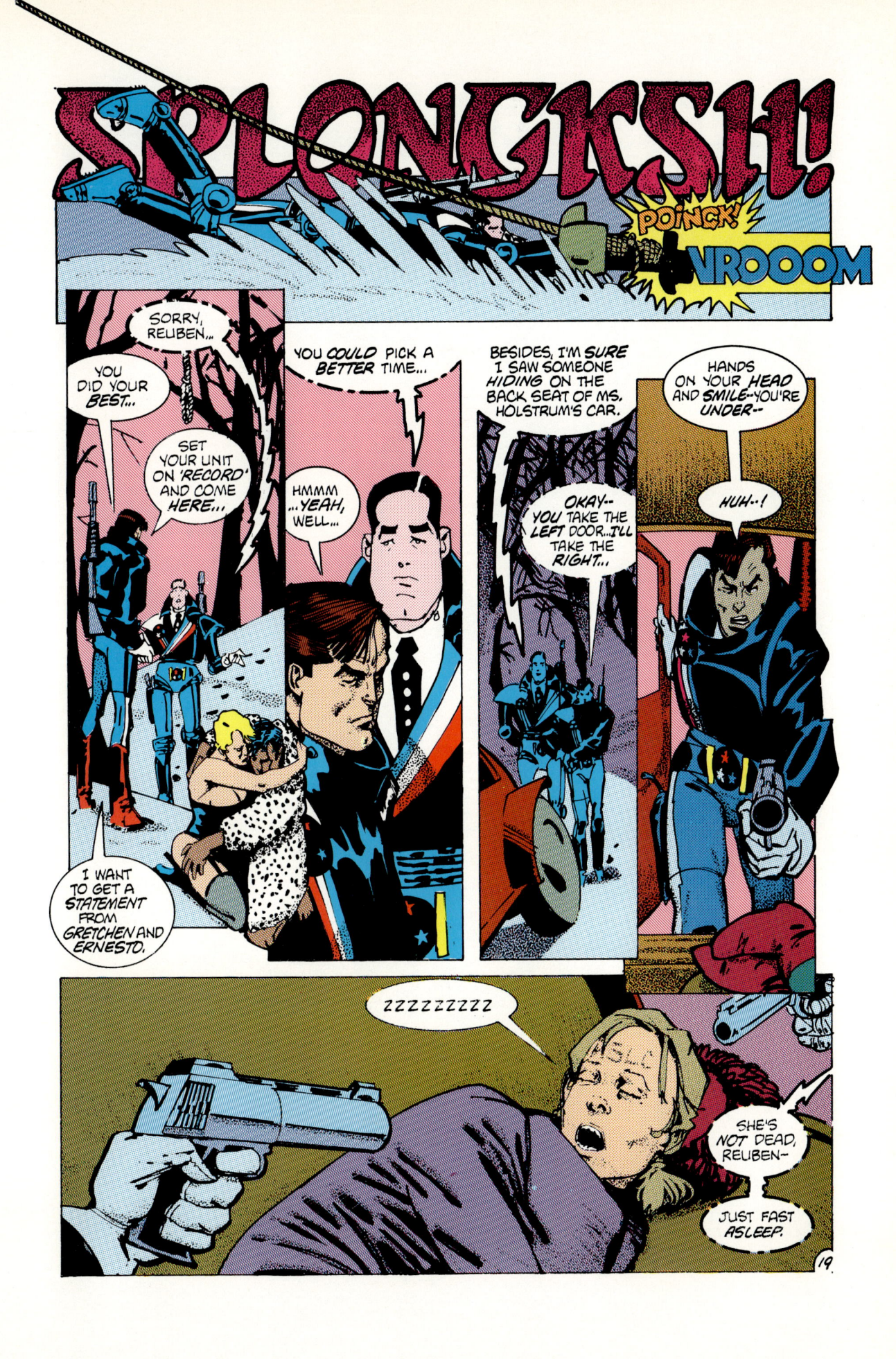

SORRY, REUBEN...

YOU DID YOUR BEST...

SET YOUR UNIT ON 'RECORD' AND COME HERE...

YOU COULD PICK A BETTER TIME...

HMMM...YEAH, WELL...

BESIDES, I'M SURE I SAW SOMEONE HIDING ON THE BACK SEAT OF MS. HOLSTRUM'S CAR.

OKAY-- YOU TAKE THE LEFT DOOR...I'LL TAKE THE RIGHT...

HANDS ON YOUR HEAD AND SMILE--YOU'RE UNDER--

HUH--!

I WANT TO GET A STATEMENT FROM GRETCHEN AND ERNESTO.

ZZZZZZZZZ

SHE'S NOT DEAD, REUBEN--

JUST FAST ASLEEP.

19

HER NAME'S AMY...
SHE HAD A SECONAL IN HER ALREADY, AND SHE'S STILL PRETTY DOPEY FROM MY ANES-THETIC...SHE'LL BE FINE IN THE MORNING...
HERE'S THE TOOTH...
WHAT KIND OF PEOPLE PUT A CYANIDE INLAY IN AN EIGHT YEAR OLD'S MOUTH, ANYHOW?
HARD TO SAY, DR. ZINNER... THANKS.
NOW...
LUTHER... YOU KNOW THAT IMPRESSION YOU DO OF ME... WHEN YOU THINK I'M NOT LOOKING?
WHY, REUBEN... I, UH--DON'T KNOW WHAT YOU'RE TALKING ABOUT...
DON'T GET COY WITH ME, PINOCCHIO...
...SEEMS TO ME THE ONLY USE YOU GET OUT OF YOUR HOLO-HEAD™ OPTION...
...IS THE RIDICULE AND CHEAP BURLESQUE...
...OF AUTHORITY FIGURES...
...THAT'S IT...
NOW, YOU STEELPLATED AIRHEAD... I WANT YOU TO BE ME AT THAT CONSOLE 'TIL I GET BACK.
SURE ...HOW COME?
I'VE GOT SOME UNDERCOVER WORK TO SEE TO... AND I MIGHT NEED AN ALIBI.
ANY SUGGESTIONS?
YEAH. KEEP THE REST OF YOU OUT OF CAMERA RANGE...
...AND DON'T USE 'INFER' WHEN YOU MEAN 'IMPLY.'

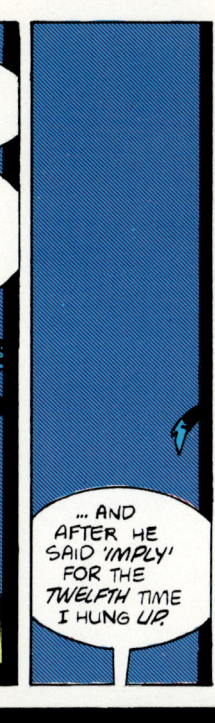

END TAPE   FAST FOR-   REWIND

"Nice of Flagg to treat us to *dinner*, Charles..."

"...Guess he's got a guilty conscience for *not* helping find Medea..."

"...He's still a *strange* duck, though..."

"I called the ranger office to *thank* him..."

"...He was obviously so doped up he couldn't sit up straight..."

"...And after he said 'imply' for the *twelfth* time I hung *up*."

"How *efficient* of Ms. de la Cristo..."

"...She's got the flight recorder all hooked to the vidunit."

"A little fast forward."

"Can't make out the markings."

"Damn. Recorder must have taken a round..."

"Better rewind it back to oops—"

"Huh!?!"

"Bojemoi!!"

"What did *that* say?"

"...ectus for transfer— land parcel, now known as the **State of Illinois,** property of Plex-USA— offered for sale to de la Cristo Land Development—a wholly- ned subsidiary of World Industries."

"...Something is *rotten* in the State of Illinois."

NEXT MORNING...
THAT'S THE WAY IT'S BEEN FOR DAYS... EVERYBODY...
...MANDY ON AIR DISPATCH... EVEN THE MAYOR'S OFFICE...
...NOBODY'S BEEN ABLE TO REACH THE PLEX...
AS I SEE IT, THERE ARE TWO POSSIBILITIES: BOTH OF WHICH STINK...
ONE--THAT de la CRISTO IS A BUNCO ARTIST PULLING SOME KIND OF SCAM...
BUZZ
YOU HAVE REACHED PLEX CENTRAL, HAMMARSKJOLD CENTER, MARS...
ALL CIRCUITS ARE BUSY. PLEASE HOLD FOR OUR NEXT AVAILABLE OPERATOR...
...OR TWO--THE PLEX IS ACTUALLY SELLING THE STATES OUT FROM UNDER US. WHAT--
MS. de la CRISTO ON LINE SIX REUBEN...
...AND AS FOR YOU, RAUL...
...SINCE YOU WANNA PLAY DUMB ANIMAL...
...LET'S SEE HOW YOU FEEL BEING TREATED LIKE ONE.
OOOOH--KITTY--
YES MS. de la CRISTO...
I'LL KILL YOU, LUTHER! I SWEAR--
I FEEL IT'S TIME TO CLEAR THE AIR ABOUT MY REQUEST TO VISIT DOWNTOWN CHICAGO...
...DINNER THIS EVENING... MY PLACE?
THANK YOU, I'LL BE THERE.
I'D SAY WE'VE GOT PLENTY TO TALK ABOUT.

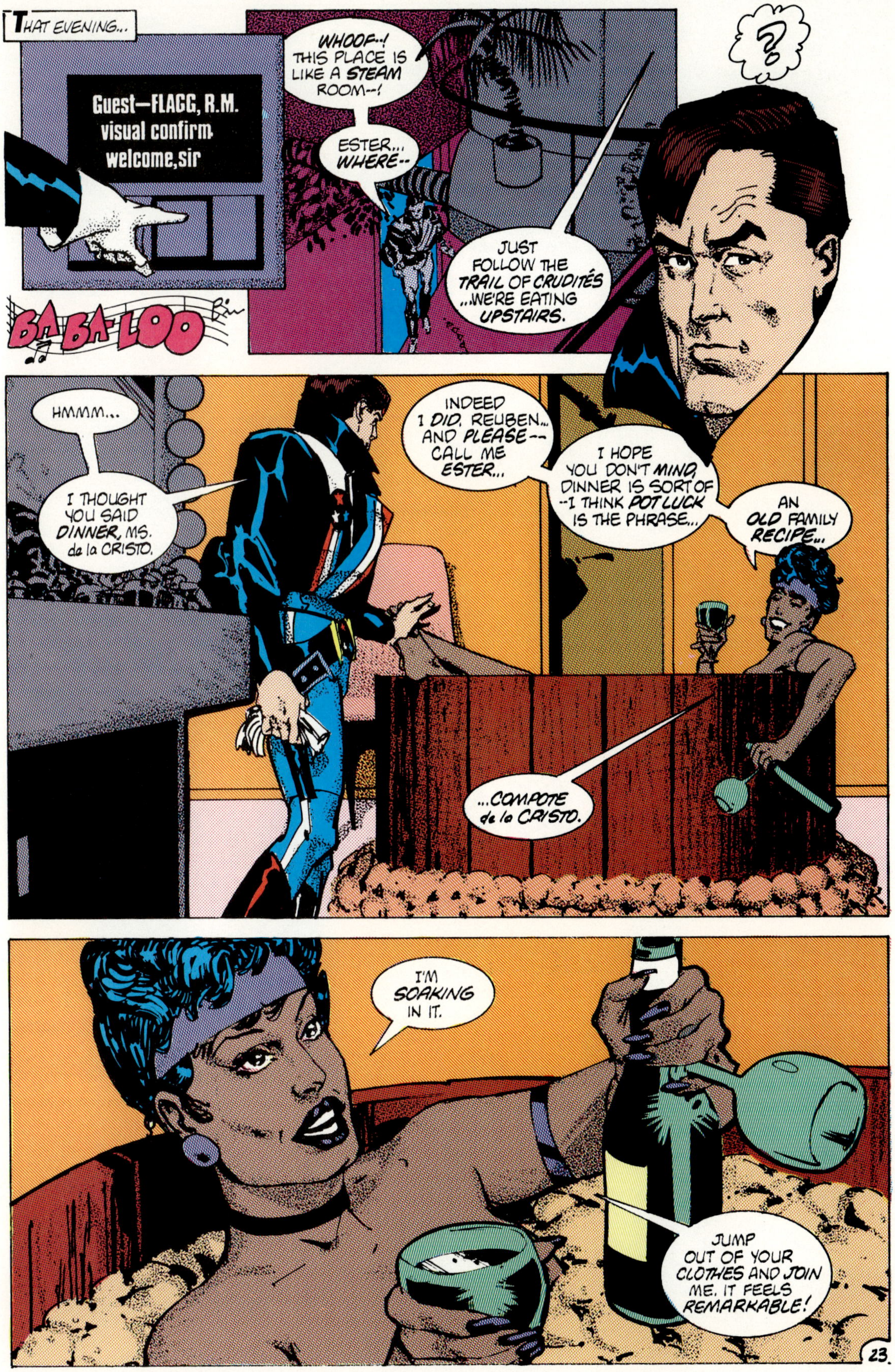
THAT EVENING...
Guest—FLAGG, R.M.
visual confirm
welcome,sir
BA-BA-LOO
WHOOF--! THIS PLACE IS LIKE A STEAM ROOM--!
ESTER... WHERE--
JUST FOLLOW THE TRAIL OF CRUDITÉS ...WE'RE EATING UPSTAIRS.
?
HMMM...
I THOUGHT YOU SAID DINNER, MS. de la CRISTO.
INDEED I DID, REUBEN... AND PLEASE-- CALL ME ESTER...
I HOPE YOU DON'T MIND. DINNER IS SORT OF --I THINK POT LUCK IS THE PHRASE...
AN OLD FAMILY RECIPE...
...COMPOTE de la CRISTO.
I'M SOAKING IN IT.
JUMP OUT OF YOUR CLOTHES AND JOIN ME. IT FEELS REMARKABLE!

Panel 1
"I'LL KEEP MY PANTS ON, THANKS..."

"AS YOU LIKE, SIT DOWN THEN, AND HELP YOURSELF..."

Panel 2
"AGAINST EVERY BETTER JUDGMENT I MUST SAY-- THIS ISN'T BAD."

"NOT BAD-- IT'S SENSATIONAL-- AND PATRIOTICALLY PAN AMERICAN, TOO!"

Panel 3
"YOU, UH-- LOOK SENSATIONAL ESTER."

"THAT'S THE BRAZILIAN PART... AFRODISIA™..."

Panel 4
"...AND FROM THE PLEXUSA--"

"--SOMNAMBUTOL™."

ZZZZZZZ

SPLASH

Panel 5
"SWEET DREAMS, SCHATZI..."

"...A QUICK HOT SHOWER TO SCRUB OFF THIS GUNK..."

Panel 6
"THEN I SUMMON ERNESTO AND THE OTHERS..."

"...AND I'M ON MY WAY."

"WITH ANY LUCK, CHICO, BY THE TIME YOU AWAKE YOU'LL BE WORKING FOR ME..."

"AND, FOR THE RECORD..."

ZZZZZZZZZZZZZZZZZZZZZZZZZZZZ

"YOU'RE FIRED."

Next morning...

"Wow— Reuben, you look *terrible*...! And you're *late*, too..."

"F.O.A.D., Luther— I'm in *no* mood."

"Have you seen de lo Cristo?"

"Sure. She rolled through here with Klein-Hernandez and a couple o' body-guards 'bout *four* this morning..."

"...picked up the keys to a *van*..."

"What?!?"

"...and went into the *city*."

"On *whose* authority?"

"*Yours* of course...! I gave 'em the *keys*— you did the *paperwork*..."

"Let me *see* that!"

"A *good* forgery... but *not* great."

"I'm *sorry*, Reuben. I guess I'm *just not familiar* enough—"

"I expect *nothing* else from *you* Luther— —you are an *idiot*."

"But Raul..."

"HE SPENT THE NIGHT IN THE LOCKUP WITH AMY..."

"...FIGURED IT MIGHT GET'M TO ACT NORMAL..."

"HOW COME HE'S SHUT UP?"

"NOBODY'S ANSWERI--"

"LUTHER, I HAVE A HEADACHE--GET ME MARSPLEX CENTRAL-PRIORITY ACCESS--"

"TRY IT AND SHUT UP--"

"⟨SNIF SNIF⟩ WHAT'S THAT SMELL?"

"YOU KNOW I HAVE NO SENSE OF SMELL..."

"...BUT-- IF YOU WANT A CHEMICAL ANALYSIS..."

"DON'T BOTHER... HMMMM..."

"SUBSTANCE IDENTIFIED AS SIPHOGENE-K... BIOLOGICAL WEAPON AFFECTING NERVOUS SYSTEMS OF HIGHER ORDERS..."

"...WITH LIMITED EFFECT ON LOWER FORMS."

"SIPHOGENE-K IS EFFECTIVE PRIMARILY AS A TOOL OF ASSASSINS..."

"...AS ITS POTENCY IS DIMINISHED BY CONTACT WITH OXYGEN..."

26

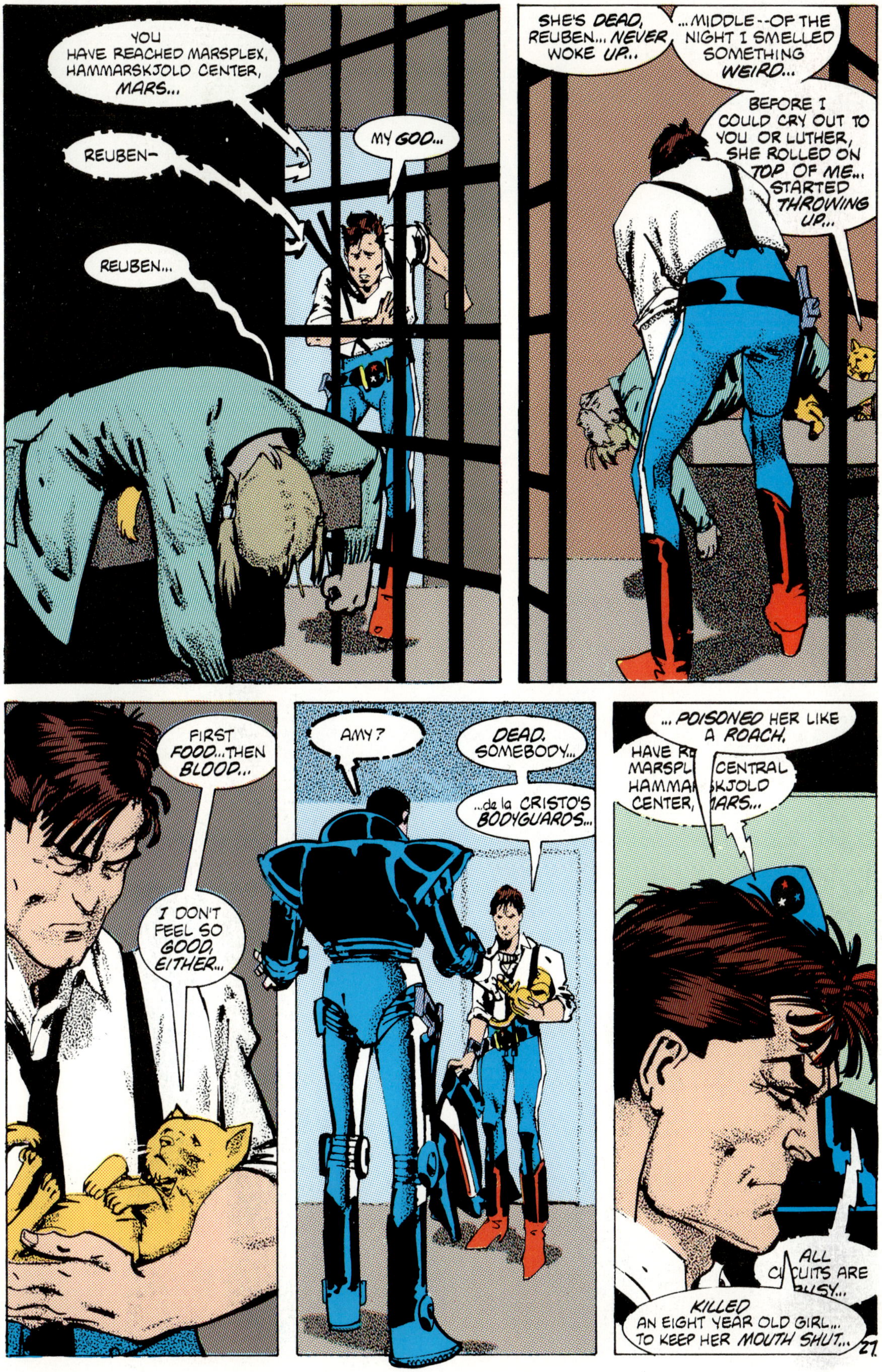

YOU HAVE REACHED MARSPLEX, HAMMARSKJOLD CENTER, MARS...
REUBEN-
REUBEN...
MY GOD...
SHE'S DEAD, REUBEN... NEVER WOKE UP...
...MIDDLE--OF THE NIGHT I SMELLED SOMETHING WEIRD...
BEFORE I COULD CRY OUT TO YOU OR LUTHER, SHE ROLLED ON TOP OF ME... STARTED THROWING UP...
FIRST FOOD...THEN BLOOD...
I DON'T FEEL SO GOOD, EITHER...
AMY?
DEAD. SOMEBODY...
...de la CRISTO'S BODYGUARDS...
...POISONED HER LIKE A ROACH.
KILLED AN EIGHT YEAR OLD GIRL... TO KEEP HER MOUTH SHUT...

28

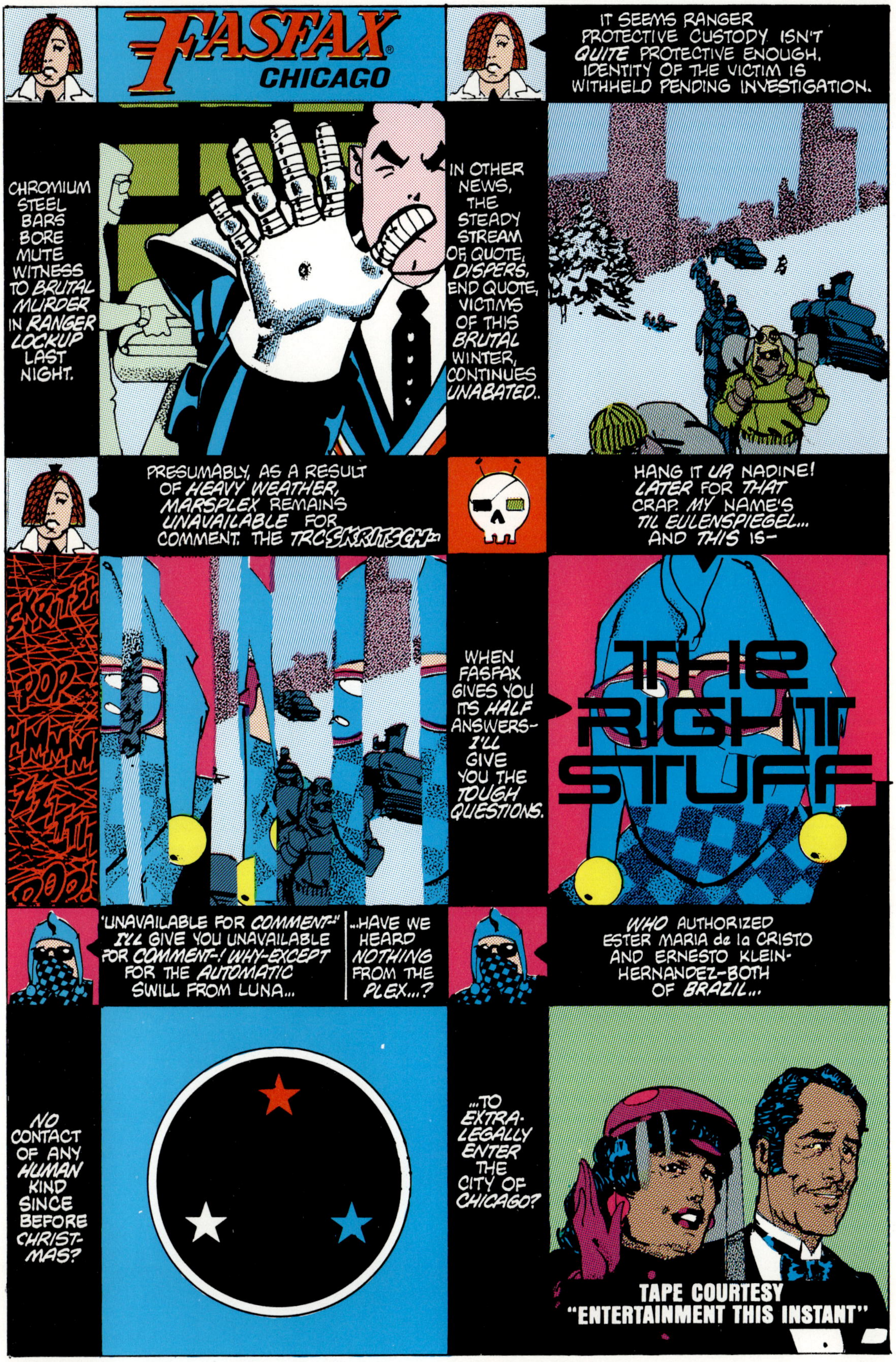
FASFAX®
CHICAGO
IT SEEMS RANGER PROTECTIVE CUSTODY ISN'T QUITE PROTECTIVE ENOUGH. IDENTITY OF THE VICTIM IS WITHHELD PENDING INVESTIGATION.
CHROMIUM STEEL BARS BORE MUTE WITNESS TO BRUTAL MURDER IN RANGER LOCKUP LAST NIGHT.
IN OTHER NEWS, THE STEADY STREAM OF, QUOTE, DISPERS, END QUOTE, VICTIMS OF THIS BRUTAL WINTER, CONTINUES UNABATED..
PRESUMABLY, AS A RESULT OF HEAVY WEATHER, MARSPLEX REMAINS UNAVAILABLE FOR COMMENT. THE TRC SKRITSCH
HANG IT UP, NADINE! LATER FOR THAT CRAP. MY NAME'S TIL EULENSPIEGEL... AND THIS IS—
WHEN FASFAX GIVES YOU ITS HALF ANSWERS— I'LL GIVE YOU THE TOUGH QUESTIONS.
THE RIGHT STUFF
'UNAVAILABLE FOR COMMENT—' I'LL GIVE YOU UNAVAILABLE FOR COMMENT—! WHY—EXCEPT FOR THE AUTOMATIC SWILL FROM LUNA...
...HAVE WE HEARD NOTHING FROM THE PLEX...?
NO CONTACT OF ANY HUMAN KIND SINCE BEFORE CHRIST-MAS?
WHO AUTHORIZED ESTER MARIA de la CRISTO AND ERNESTO KLEIN-HERNANDEZ—BOTH OF BRAZIL...
...TO EXTRA-LEGALLY ENTER THE CITY OF CHICAGO?
TAPE COURTESY "ENTERTAINMENT THIS INSTANT"

WHAT IS THE CONNECTION BETWEEN THESE TWO ALIEN NATIONALS AND THE UNDERGROUND PARAMILITARY ORGANIZATION CALLED--
WHAT?... WE, UH--SEEM TO BE EXPERIENCING SOME TECHNICAL DIFFICULTIES--SO THIS IS IT 'TIL NEXT TIME--
KAA BOOM
A.S.L.C.
American Survivalist Labor Committee
WHAT THE BLOODY HELL WAS THAT?
SPINK!
FASFAX APOLOGIZES FOR THE OFFENSIVE INTERRUPTION OF OUR PROGRAMMING...
IF THE RANGERS ADDED COMPETENCE TO THEIR REPERTOIRE, WE MIGHT NOT HAVE TO ENDURE SUCH ACTS OF PIRACY...
OKAY, LUTHER-- WHAT GIVES?
YOUR HONOR--MS. HOLSTRUM--IT'S THE TRUTH. MS. de la CRISTO FORGED REUBEN'S SIGNATURE ON A DOWNTOWN VISA--
--SHE CAME THROUGH HERE WITH MR. KLEIN-HERNANDEZ AND HER BODYGUARDS AT ABOUT FOUR A.M...
...WHILE I CHECKED THE PAPER WORK, SOMEBODY STUCK A NERVE GAS PELLET UNDER THE LOCKUP DOOR...
OH, GOD--
WHERE'S REUBEN AND RAUL?
2

RAUL TOOK A DOSE OF THE NERVE GAS... HE'S AT THE VET...

...REUBEN'S ON HIS WAY DOWNTOWN.

THIS COULD MEAN AN INTERNATIONAL INCIDENT...

...WITH MS. de la CRISTO AND MR. KLEIN-HERNANDEZ CHARGED AS ACCESSORIES TO MURDER...

IN THE CASE OF THAT BITCH, YOU CAN THROW AWAY THE ACCESSORY...

WAIT'LL YOU SEE THE PRESENTATION WE GOT—THE SET ON THE BLONDE'LL KILL—

WHAT'S HIS ETA?

I'LL DO THAT MS. HOLSTRUM.

...BUT ERNESTO'S GOT TO BE INNOCENT.

PLEASE-- CALL ME IF YOU HEAR ANYTHING.

"HE SMUGGLING IN THE FIREPOWER WITH DR. WEIS ON THE NOON BULLET FROM PEORIA."

I STILL DON'T UNDERSTAND WHY WE HAD TO TAKE A TRAIN, DR. WEIS.

KRIEGER PLEXMALL IN FIVE MINUTES-- LAST STOP--

AS I EXPLAINED TO YOUR MR. DECKER...

--CHECK OVERHEAD RACKS FOR CARRY ON LUGGAGE AND PERSONAL BELONGINGS...

3

ALL THOSE TRIPS TO JERRY RIGG™ FOR THE ASSEMBLY OF *YOUR* PROSTHETICS...

HAVE *DEPLETED* MY FUEL ALLOWANCE TO NEAR *ZIP*.

SO *WHAT?* YOU'LL BE *REIMBURSED.*

IT'LL TAKE *MONTHS*--YOU KNOW *THAT*--

BESIDES, I HAD *NO* DESIRE TO CLEAR AWAY HALF MY PORTABLE SURGERY TO MAKE ROOM FOR OUR 'BAGGAGE'!

OKAY... YOU'VE MADE YOUR POINT.

C'MON--WE'RE ALMOST *IN*--LET ME GIVE YOU A *HAND*...

THANKS, IT'LL BE A PLEASURE TO *NOT NEED* THE HAND... JUST A *FEW* MORE HOURS, THEN--

HOLY--

LOOK--IT'S *HIM*--!

WHAT-- WHERE--?

I MEAN *REALLY*, BILL-- --*TIL EULENSPIEGEL?*

I WISH YOU'D CLEARED IT WITH *ME*--

WHAT'S ALL THE *COMMOTION?*

THERE'S AN *ASSAULT PISTOL* IN MY CARRY ON-- LET--

ARE YOU *CRAZY?!?* NOT *HERE*--!

STATE
HOWARD CHAYKIN'S
AMERICAN FLAGG!
HE'S GETTING AWAY-!
HE'LL BE BACK. YOU'LL HAVE PLENTY OF TIME TO KILL HIM LATER.
AGAIN, BILL. I MISSED THAT.
I SAID, WE'RE CAUGHT IN THE MIDDLE OF A FIREFIGHT--TWO JEWISH OFFENSE BRIGADIERS ARE THROWING FIRE FROM THE EL...
ILLEGAL ASSAULT IN A NON-COMBAT ZONE...
THAT'S ONE FELONY...
of the UNION
conclusion

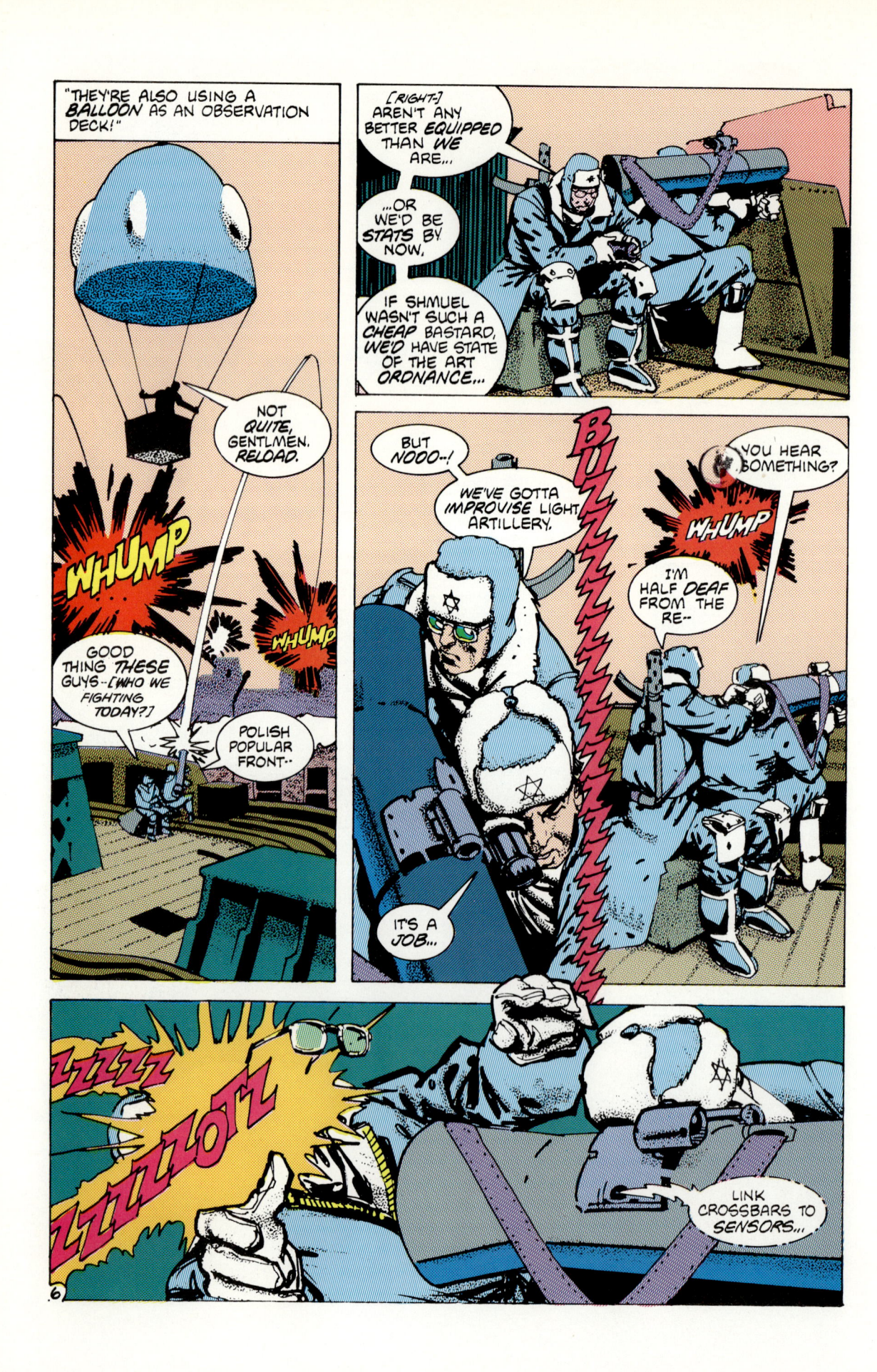

"THEY'RE ALSO USING A *BALLOON* AS AN OBSERVATION DECK!"

[RIGHT-] AREN'T ANY BETTER *EQUIPPED* THAN *WE* ARE...

...OR WE'D BE *STATS* BY NOW.

IF SHMUEL WASN'T SUCH A *CHEAP* BASTARD, WE'D HAVE STATE OF THE ART *ORDNANCE*...

NOT *QUITE*, GENTLEMEN. RELOAD.

GOOD THING *THESE* GUYS--[WHO WE FIGHTING TODAY?]

POLISH POPULAR FRONT--

BUT *NOOO*--! WE'VE GOTTA *IMPROVISE* LIGHT ARTILLERY.

YOU HEAR *SOMETHING*?

I'M HALF *DEAF* FROM THE *RE*--

IT'S A *JOB*...

LINK CROSSBARS TO SENSORS...

ZOTZ?!?

LOCK SENSOR TO *TARGET*...

ZZZZZZZZZZZZZZZOT!

FIRE!

I SAID *FIRE!*

WHAT'S WITH YOU TWO *PUTZES*—

...THEY'RE MOVING THEIR EMPLACEMENT..

..THEY'RE FULLY *EXPOSED*...

FIRE! DAMNIT--

7.

WHUMP! KABOOOOM!!!

"FIRE!"

"AN EIGHT YEAR OLD GIRL?"

"THAT'S RIGHT, HARRIS."

"WHILE I LAY DOPED UP ON SOMNAMBUTOL™..."

"...de la CRISTO, KLEIN-HERNANDEZ AND THEIR BODYGUARDS PITSTOPPED AT THE STATION TO MURDER A CHILD..."

"...THEN DROVE DOWNTOWN."

"ANY PROGRESS ON PINPOINTING THEIR WHEREABOUTS?"

"WE SHOULD HAVE IT IN A MOMENT..."

"DID YOU GET ANYTHING ON ASLC INTERROGATING THE KID?"

"NEVER GOT THE CHANCE...WHAT WITH THE DISPERS AND THE DIRIGIBLE CRASH--"

"HERE'S THE DATA YOU WANTED, REUBEN--"

8

MANDY!?
THERE'S A COUNCIL OF WARLORDS AT THE LIGHTNING BAR... ON KENMORE...
SPONSORED BY "THE COMMITTEE FOR A NEW BRASILIA"...
...CHAIRPERSON OF "THE COMMITTEE" IS ESTER MARIA de la CRISTO.
THANKS.
THE LIGHTNING'S A PRETTY RUGGED JOINT...AMBIENCE à la LITTLE BIG HORN...
YOU NEED A BACKUP...?
DON'T BOTHER.
JUST STAY HERE AND KEEP TRYING TO CHISEL A PIECE OF THIS STATION...
REUBEN, THAT'S UNFAIR--!
JUST LIKE LIFE.
ANY IDEA WHY de la CRISTO'S SO HOT TO SEE CHICAGO?
OH, YEAH...
YOU'D BE ALL HOT AND BOTHERED TO VISIT CHICAGO TOO...
IF YOU'D JUST TRADED AN UNIMAGINABLE TONNAGE OF PRECIOUS METAL...
SNIK
VRRROOM
...IN EXCHANGE FOR THE LAND RIGHTS, TITLES AND DEEDS...
TO THE STATE OF ILLINOIS.

JERRY RIGG CUSTOM
THANK YOU, DR. WEIS --COME AGAIN.
EACH SEGMENT HAS BEEN INDIVIDUALLY TESTED...
...AND THE ASSEMBLED UNITS HAVE BEEN GIVEN A PUNISHING RUN THROUGH...
YOU'RE SURE THESE'LL HOLD ME...? I'VE PUT ON SOME WEIGHT...
THEY'LL BE FINE.
HOWEVER, I'LL ONLY AGREE TO ATTACH THEM TODAY IF YOU GIVE ME YOUR WORD AS AN OFFICER...
...THAT THERE'LL BE NO REPEATS OF THAT OUTBURST ON THE TRAIN.
PROMISE. I'M AWFULLY SORRY...
...IT'S--IT'S JUST THE SIGHT OF HIM...
YES...?
Love Canal Adult Center
ENTRANCE AROUND CORNER
THE ABIDING PASSION OF MY LIFE IS TO SLOWLY AND PAINFULLY MURDER REUBEN FLAGG...
I TELL YOU, CRYSTAL, I DON'T KNOW WHAT TO DO...
BOOM BOOM ROO
IT'S NO GREAT COMFORT... BUT THIS ISN'T THE FIRST TIME ERNESTO'S BEEN DRAGGED THROUGH THE MUD BY de la CRISTO...
HELLO, LADIES--MAY I JOIN YOU?
WITH ANY LUCK IT'LL BE THE LAST...
CIGARS... CIGARETTES... SEXUAL APPLIANCES...
...THEN TO SLAUGHTER, COOK AND EAT HIS DAMNED CAT.
I MEAN...
I KNOW WHAT YOU MEAN, CRYSTAL. THANKS.

I'VE GOT TO SHOW MY FACE AT MY CONSOLE-- TAKE THE WHEEL, EH, C.K.?
NO SWEAT.
THANKS, CRYSTAL...
...YOU'VE BEEN SEEING de la CRISTO, HAVEN'T YOU, C.K.?
SURE. JUST FUN STUFF-- NOTHING HEAVY.
BUT FROM WHAT I HEAR ABOUT YOU AND ERNESTO... I MEAN, GRETCHEN--
ERNESTO'S A HIGH-RANKING BRAZILIAN DIPLOMAT, AND MARRIED--
AND YOU--WELL, YOU-
I KNOW WHAT I AM, C.K.
I'VE BEEN COMMERCIAL FOR SO LONG, I THOUGHT I'D OUTGROWN INTIMACY...
BUT-- ERNESTO--DAMN IT!
HE'S A SENSATIONAL MAN. HE MAKES ME VIBRATE...
I--I THINK I LOVE HIM. THERE!
OH, COME ON, GRET, DON'T BE--
I MEAN IT, CHARLIE--I-- OH, GOD--
THIS IS KILLING ME.
SNIF
CHARLIE?
11.

THIS BAR-- IN FACT, THIS ENTIRE TURF ZONE SECTOR-
--IS OFF LIMITS TO ALL BUT REGISTERED POLI-CLUB PERSONNEL.
NO EXCEPTIONS?
NONE--'SPECIALLY NOT FOR NO PLEXUS RANGER--
SO BEAT--
SNIK!
IT! HEY-WHAT--
ZZZZZZZLOTZ
UCCHK!

'NOTHER BLACK AND BLUE OVER HERE, MITCH--
I MEAN, LOOK AT THIS GUT-EATHER HOLDS OUT MUCH ONGER, WE'LL ALL BE FAT AS PIGS!
'YOU SEE FIREFIGHT LAST NIGHT?
EAH--SNUCK IN ERUN FOR OUR POT--
TAYA 'SPECT? NO ACTION IN WO MONTHS...
OT SINCE YOUNG LOR BIT IT--
CREEEAK...
SLAM!!
I NEED SOME ANSWERS-- NOW!
HOW IN HELL'D HE GET IN HERE?
YO, FRANK-- HE TOOK DOWN SONNY AND FELIX--!
I DON'T WANT TROUBLE... I WANT THE WOMAN WHO SPONSORED THIS GET-TOGETHER...
AND HER BODY GU--
FORGET IT, WUSS--YOU KNOW THE RULES...
RANGERS GOT NO MUSCLE IN A WAR ZONE--
C'MON, TRIF-- DON'T BUST CHOPS--
DROP DEAD, FRANK--
LOOK, I DON'T NEED A HARD TIME. THIS IS A HOMICIDE INVESTIGATION...
ALL YOU GET FROM ME IS NAME, RANK AND SERIAL NUMBER... HAW!
13

THAT'S PUCINSKI, TRIFON V., FIELD MARSHAL, GLOW BOYS, NUMBER 604-24-8200.
COMLINK DATAMAX-- HOW MAY I HELP YOU?
SNIKIT
PUCINSKI, TRIFON VALENTIN FIELD MARSHAL GLOW BOYS 602-24-8200
FLAGG, R.M. ACCESS CODE 479-- OUTSTANDING INDICTMENTS?
MAY SEVEN, '28--ESPIONAGE... MARCH ONE, '29--RIVER PIRACY AND ILLEGAL BLOCKADE RUNNING...
HEY, TRIF--I NEVER KNEW YOU GOT RAPPED FOR SPYING...
YEAH-- I WAS STILL A SHABBOS GOY BACK THEN--
--BEAT THE RAP BY KILLING THE REF.
...ASSASIN-ATION OF JUDGES...
THOSE ARE MILITARY--
KLIK KLIK KLIK KLIK KLIK
ANYTHING CIVIL?
...RAPE?
BLAM
14

NOW--ARE THERE ANY MORE CANDIDATES FOR HAREM GUARD...
...OR DO I START GETTING SOME CO-OPERATION?
KRASH!
MAYBE I OVERESTIMATED THE SHOCK VALUE OF--
HANDS ON YOUR HEADS, LADIES AND GENTS...
...OR YOU'RE ALL STEAK TARTARE.
YOU MAY PROCEED, RANGER...
THANK YOU.
--YOU-- TALK TO ME--
PEOPLE YOU WANT BEEN HERE AND GONE.
DIDN'T LOOK LIKE BODYGUARD AND CLIENT TO ME...
YEAH?
KIDNAPPER AND VICTIM'S MORE LIKE IT.
KEEP TALKING...

The COMMITTEE for a NEW BRASILIA invites you to a seminar- "Mocambo-American Spiritualism for the 21st Century?" Open Bar Dress: unarmed
LET'S FACE IT--ALL THIS SNOW HAS REALLY STOPPED THE ACTION...
...AND WITH ALL THE STORES AND RESTAURANTS SHUT DOWN, THERE'S NO LOOTING... OR SPONSORS... OR INSURANCE...
...WE'RE ALL FREAKING OUT FROM CABIN FEVER...
THIS SEEMED LIKE A GOOD WAY TO GET TOGETHER-UNDER TRUCE...HAVE SOME LAUGHS...
THEN THESE WOODCHUCKS CAME IN LIKE THEY OWNED THE PLACE WITH THIS CHICK IN CUFFS, RIGHT...?
THAT DIDN'T SIT REAL WELL WITH THE WIVES...
...THEN THESE RUBES OFFERED TO LET US, YOU KNOW... LIKE...PLAY THROUGH...
...THAT REALLY TICKED THE WOMEN OFF.
BUT THE LAST STRAW WAS WHEN THE HEAD RUBE STARTED MAKIN' A SPIEL FOR SOME SURVIVAL COMMITTEE...
...HANDING OUT PAMPHLETS...
...BUT ONLY TO THE WHITE GUYS...
...WE MAY HATE EACH OTHER'S GUTS IN COMBAT...
... BUT WE DON'T NEED SOME SMARTASS HICK STIRRING UP ANY MORE TENSION...
...THEY BEAT IT, PRONTO...
...ONE OF THE NEUTRAL O.P.'S REPORTED SIGHTING THEM HEADING NORTHWEST...
WHAT THE HELL COULD THEY WANT...

"...IN HEADHUNTER TERRITORY?"

WHERE'S HE TAKING ERNESTO?

HE HAS TO TAKE A--

I TOLD YOU WE SHOULD'VE TURNED LEFT.

YOU'RE NOT LIKE THE OTHERS, WARREN...YOU'RE GENTLE...

THANK YOU, MA'AM...

ESTER...

WE CAN STILL MAKE THE RENDEZVOUS...

BUT I DON'T HAVE TO...

ANYWAY, WE'VE GOT THE DYNAMITE.

DID YOU AUTHORIZE THAT?

HUH...?

OH--STEVE'S BEEN PRETTY HUFFED SINCE HE DROPPED TROU AND SHE LAUGHED IN HIS FACE...

...HE'S JUST BLOWING OFF SOME STEAM...

...I MEAN, WE NEED de la CRISTO FOR THE RANSOM...

KLIK KLIK

BLAM

...BUT WHAT'S ONE SPICK BUREAUCRAT IN THE SCHEME OF THINGS?

SNIK SNIK

WHAT WAS--

WHOOOOOOOOSH

HOLY CHRIST-- NAPALM!

WE BEEN AMBUSHED!

GET US OUT OF HERE!

17

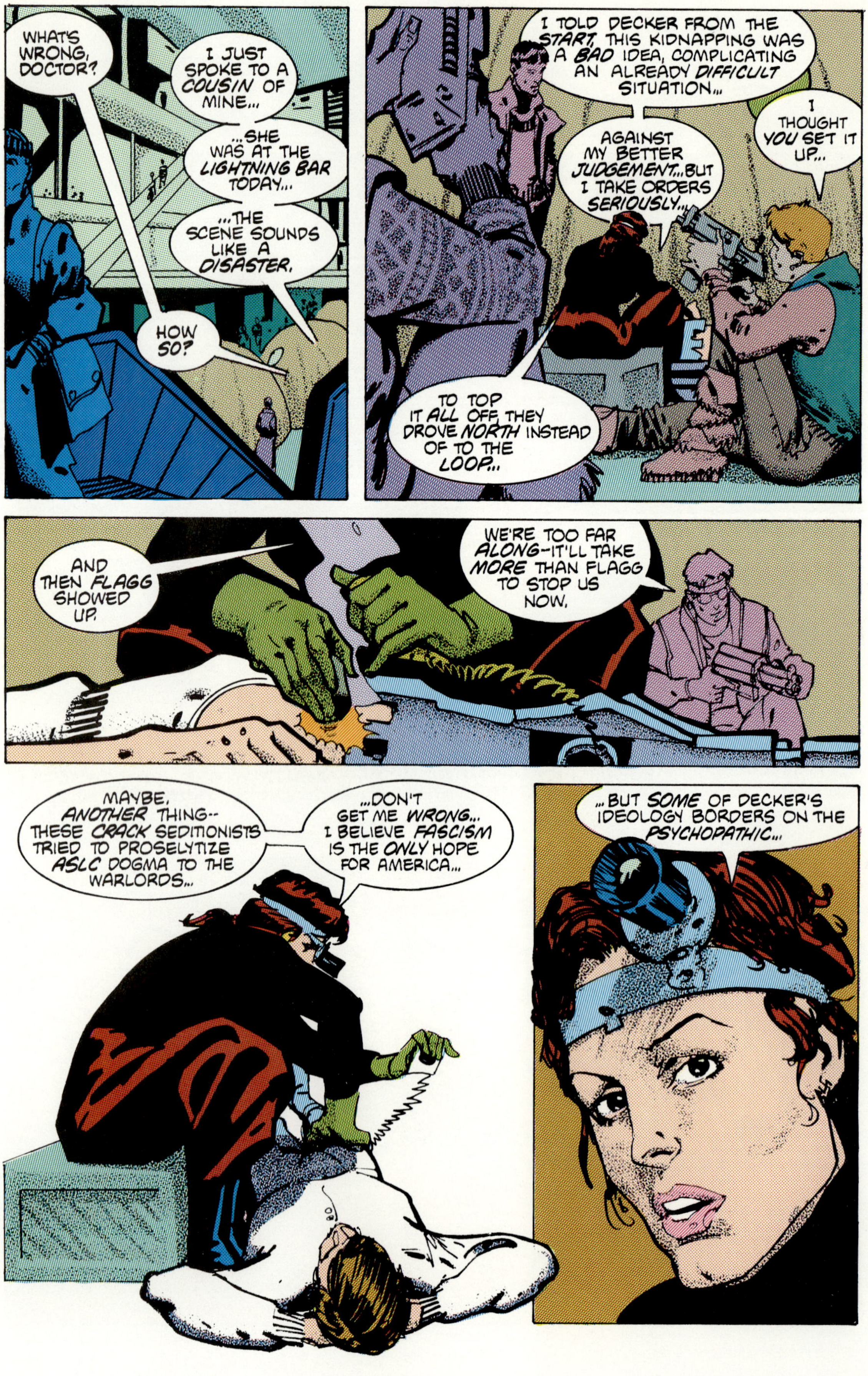
WHAT'S WRONG, DOCTOR?
I JUST SPOKE TO A COUSIN OF MINE...
...SHE WAS AT THE LIGHTNING BAR TODAY...
...THE SCENE SOUNDS LIKE A DISASTER.
HOW SO?
I TOLD DECKER FROM THE START, THIS KIDNAPPING WAS A BAD IDEA, COMPLICATING AN ALREADY DIFFICULT SITUATION...
AGAINST MY BETTER JUDGEMENT...BUT I TAKE ORDERS SERIOUSLY...
I THOUGHT YOU SET IT UP...
TO TOP IT ALL OFF THEY DROVE NORTH INSTEAD OF TO THE LOOP...
AND THEN FLAGG SHOWED UP.
WE'RE TOO FAR ALONG--IT'LL TAKE MORE THAN FLAGG TO STOP US NOW.
MAYBE, ANOTHER THING-- THESE CRACK SEDITIONISTS TRIED TO PROSELYTIZE ASLC DOGMA TO THE WARLORDS...
...DON'T GET ME WRONG... I BELIEVE FASCISM IS THE ONLY HOPE FOR AMERICA...
...BUT SOME OF DECKER'S IDEOLOGY BORDERS ON THE PSYCHOPATHIC...

I COULDN'T AGREE MORE...
DECKER IS COMPLETELY CRAZED.
FEELING BETTER, RAUL?
OH YEAH-- THANKS, CRYSTAL.
VET SAID I GOTTA STAY AWAY FROM VODKA A WHILE...
THAT'S PRECISELY WHY I TALKED HIM OUT OF RUNNING THIS SHOW HIMSELF...
...AND LETTING ME HANDLE IT.
SLOWLY, JOHN...
DON'T WORRY-- THEY FEEL FINE...
DECKER MAY THINK HE'S IN CHARGE...
...BUT I'M HERE.
AND IF YOU GUYS ARE AS SMART AS YOU LOOK...
...YOU'LL STICK WITH ME.
MOTHER 'O PEARL...!
TO HELL WITH DOCTOR'S ORDERS
I NEED A DRINK...
...I'M HALLUCINATING DEAD MEN.

REUBEN, YOU REALLY ARE AN IDIOT.
GOING IN THERE ALONE WAS STUPID ENOUGH...
...BUT SHOOTING A FIELD MARSHAL IN THE CROTCH--! COME ON!
MANDY--
MANDY-- I SAID--
I TOLD YOU IT WAS A DANGEROUS JOINT BACK AT BILL'S...OH.
WHAT--?
NOW I GET IT.
YOU WERE JUST PLAYING THE COMPLETE TURD BECAUSE I'D SPENT THE NIGHT WITH BILL.
DON'T BE SILLY--I WASN'T
YES YOU WERE-
NO, I--
WERE-
WELL--A LITTLE...
THAT'S ALL I WANTED TO HEAR.
YOU CAN GO TO HELL--AND I DON'T LIKE BEING CALLED A CHISELER, EITHER.
NOW-- WHAT'S ALL THIS ABOUT ESTER BUYING CHICAGO?
WELL-
YOU SMELL SOMETHING?
SNIFF- SNIFF- YEAH--
GASOLINE-- OR NAPALM--

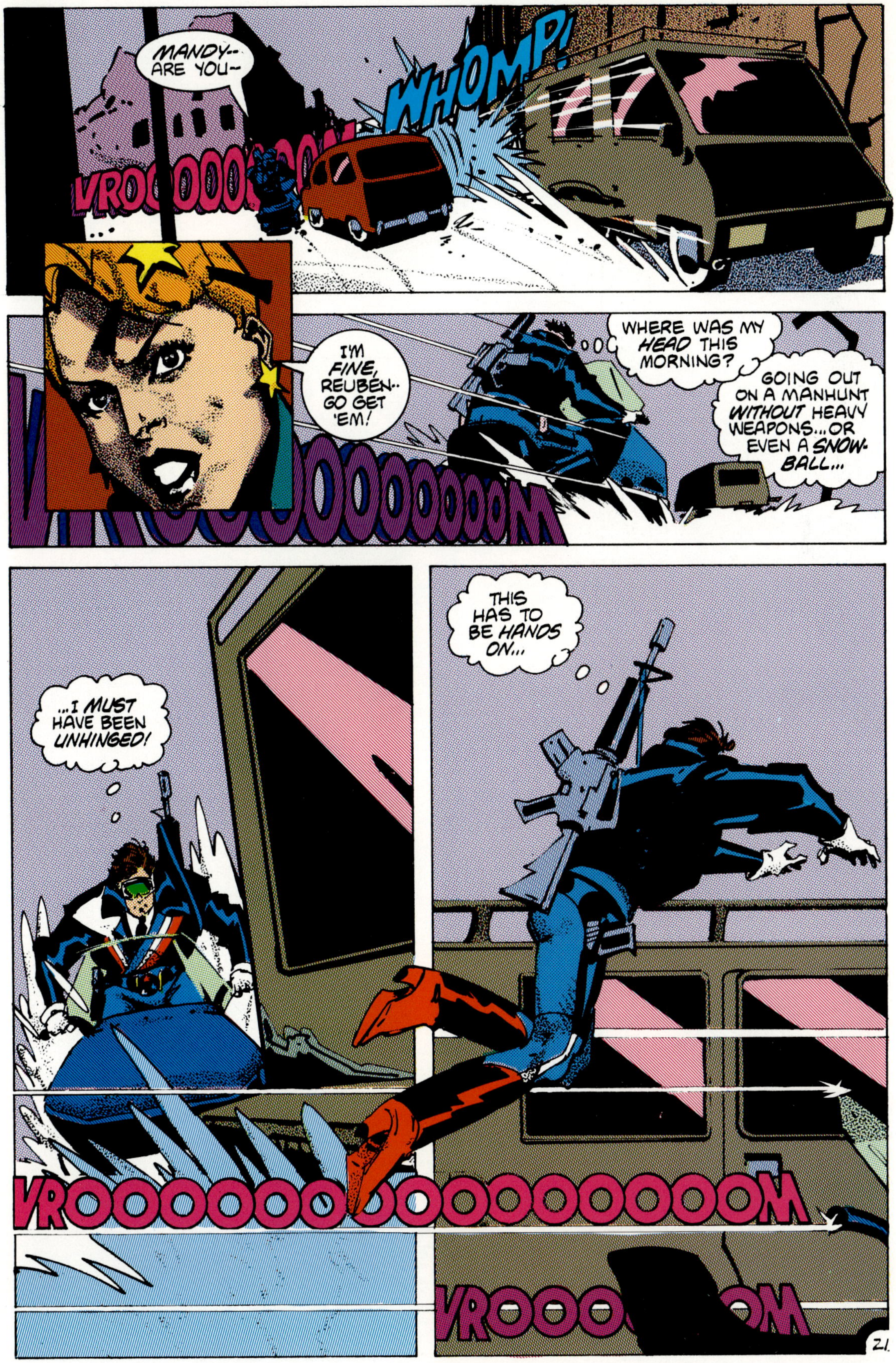
MANDY-- ARE YOU--
WHOMP!
VROOOOOOOOM
I'M FINE, REUBEN.. GO GET 'EM!
WHERE WAS MY HEAD THIS MORNING?
GOING OUT ON A MANHUNT WITHOUT HEAVY WEAPONS...OR EVEN A SNOWBALL...
VROOOOOOOOOOOOM
...I MUST HAVE BEEN UNHINGED!
THIS HAS TO BE HANDS ON...
VROOOOOOOOOOOOOOOOOOM
VROOOOOOM

UNNGH!
SO THAT'S WHY NO GUNPLAY--
IT'S JUST A DRIVER AND ESTER?!?
SO--
KRAKSH
-JUMP, ESTER--
AAARGH!
BUT--
I SAID JUMP, DAMN IT--
IT'S OUT OF...
...CONTROL!
KRASH!!
VROOOOOOOOM
VROOOOOOO
NO!

KAT-A-THA-
FLAGG-YOU STUPID BASTARD--!
BOOM!!
I'M GOING TO HAVE TO BRING YOU IN FOR QUESTIONING AS AN ACCESSORY TO MURDER...
WHOSE MURDER? SCREW YOU! I'VE GOT DIPLOMATIC CREDENTIALS...
WE'LL SEE.
EVERYTHING WAS FINE UNTIL YOU STUCK YOUR NOSE IN...
...YOUR DAMNED PLEX TRIED TO RIP ME OFF...
BUT I HAD IT ALL ON TAPE... RECORDS, DEEDS, CURRENCY TRANSFERS... EVERYTHING...
...DAMNIT, I OWNED ALL OF ILLINOIS AND ANYTHING I WANTED OF INDIANA...
NOW, THANKS TO YOU, ALL THOSE RECORDS ARE SO MUCH PLASTIC SLAG IN THE CHICAGO RIVER...
TOUGH BREAK...
23

WHERE IS AMBASSADOR KLEIN-HERNANDEZ?

CAN YOU LEAD US BACK TO HIS BODY?

SHOT IN THE BACK OF THE HEAD...

BODY...?

AFTER THAT NAPALM AMBUSH, YOU'LL NEED A SIFTER TO COLLECT WHAT'S LEFT....

CAN WE GO NOW? I'M FREEZING.

COLD BLOODED BITCH.

MOMENTS LATER...

I HAD THAT TOOTHLESS, STUPID DEGENERATE RIGHT WHERE I WANTED HIM...

...IT WAS LIKE HE'D NEVER SEEN A WOMAN IN HIS LIFE...

...THEN YOU HAD TO COME ALONG AND BRAIN HIM.

I EVEN CONVINCED HIM TO DRIVE ME BACK TO THE MALL...

...INSTEAD OF RENDEZVOUSING WITH HIS PALS AT SOME DOWNTOWN FLESH BAR...

FLESH BAR?

THAT'S WHAT THE EXPLOSIVES WERE FOR...

SOME NONSENSE ABOUT THE KING OF ENGLAND WORKING IN A TOPLESS JOINT.

OH MY GOD--

24

THEY GOT BILL...
SOON'S THE LIGHTS WENT DOWN FOR THE FIRST SHOW, THEY OPENED FIRE...
HOW'D THEY GET THROUGH YOUR DOOR CHECK? FAKE I.D.?
IT WASN'T A.S.L.C...
...THEY WERE REGULARS... GOTTERDAMMERCRATS... BEEN DRINKING HERE FOR YEARS.
WE LOST THREE PEOPLE... INCLUDING MY BEST DANCER...
...BUT WE MANAGED TO CUT DOWN HALF OF 'EM BEFORE THEY GOT AWAY.
SO NOW WE KNOW THE 'DAMMERCRATS ARE IN LEAGUE WITH A.S.L.C...
THIS IS A SPECIAL FORECAST FROM KRIEGER PLEXMALL...
I COULD HAVE TOLD YOU THAT. I FOUND MY BODYGUARDS THROUGH THAT GOTTERDAM-MERCRAT DOCTOR WHO'S ALWAYS AT THE MALL...
MY NAME IS TITANIA WEIS...
THAT'S HER--
HUH?!?
A REWARD OF 25,000 INTERCREDS IS OFFERED FOR INFOMATION LEADING TO THE ARREST OF FORMER PLEXUS RANGER REUBEN FLAGG...

...FLAGG IS CHARGED WITH MURDER, CONSPIRACY AND TREASON AGAINST THE PEOPLE OF THE UNITED STATES...
..MORE ON THAT LATER... NOW LET'S JOIN MARTIN FLOTSKY, LIVE IN THE MALL...
THANK YOU, DR. WEIS...
...WE'RE HERE AT THE RANGER STATION WITH THE MAN OF THE HOUR...
NOW, AS I WAS SAYING, MARTY,...
...DO WE REALLY WANT AN AMERICA POLICED BY ROBOTS?
HEY-- WHAT?
ESPECIALLY ROBOTS EASIER TO DEACTIVATE THAN A VIDUNIT?
URNGLE
PING
PING
HOLD DOWN THE FORT HERE, BUTCH--I GOTTA MAKE A SPEECH...
SPINK
YOU BET, BIG GUY--GIVE 'EM HELL--
AS A MAN WHO SERVED THE PLEX FOR YEARS, I CAN STATE IT AS A FACT...
...WE'VE LET TECHNOLOGY RUN OUR LIVES FOR TOO LONG.
IT'S TIME TO GET BACK TO BASICS...
BACK UP, BUDDY--
HELLO, YOUR HONOR...

YOU!?!

...BUT FOR *NOW*, LET'S GO TO PAVILLION *ONE* ON THE *MAIN* CONCOURSE...

...WHERE MALL DWELLERS AND DISPERS ARE GATHERED *TOGETHER*...

WE'LL BE BACK FOR *FURTHER* COMMENT ON TONIGHT'S EVENTS FROM HIS HONOR, *CHARLES K. BLITZ*...

...LET'S *TALK* TO SOME OF THEM...

WHAT'S *YOUR* IMPRESSION OF TONIGHT'S EVENTS?

WELL, I'VE *READ* THIS... *A.S.L.C.?* LEAFLET, AND IT MAKES *A LOT* OF SENSE TO ME...

THANK YOU, FRIENDS.

WE'RE HERE TO *STOP* THIS COUNTRY'S SLIDE INTO *OBLIVION*...

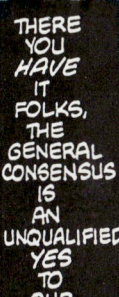

THERE YOU *HAVE* IT FOLKS, THE GENERAL CONSENSUS IS AN UNQUALIFIED YES TO OUR *NEW* PLEXUS RANGER John Scheiskopf!

..."A *CRISIS PRECIPITATED* BY THE *MOST MALEVOLENT* CRIMINAL CARTEL KNOWN TO MAN...

...THE *ITALO-BRIT-ZIONIST* CONSPIRACY.

...AND WHEN *GERMANY* NUKED *LONDON*, WE ALL THOUGHT IT WAS *GOOD BYE* TO THE ROYAL FAMILY.

WE WERE WRONG.

THE *ZIONISTS* GOT *VAPORIZED* BY *IRAN* IN '96...

THE *PAN-AFRIQUES* ATE THE *POPE* IN '04 (chuckle)...

SO, TO SET THINGS *RIGHT*, ON FEBRUARY 22, TO HONOR THE BIRTHDAY OF OUR *FIRST* PRESIDENT...

27

WE WILL BROADCAST, LIVE, THE TRIAL, CONVICTION AND EXECUTION...
...OF THE KING OF ENGLAND.
AND REUBEN FLAGG... IF YOU'RE WATCHING...
...YOU'RE NEXT.
THE END

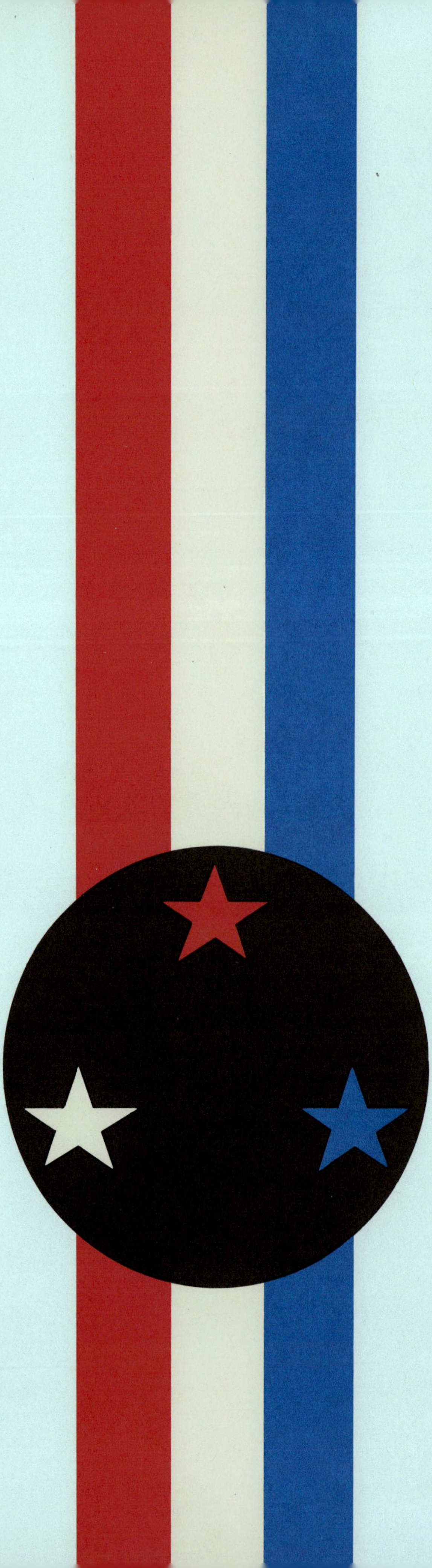

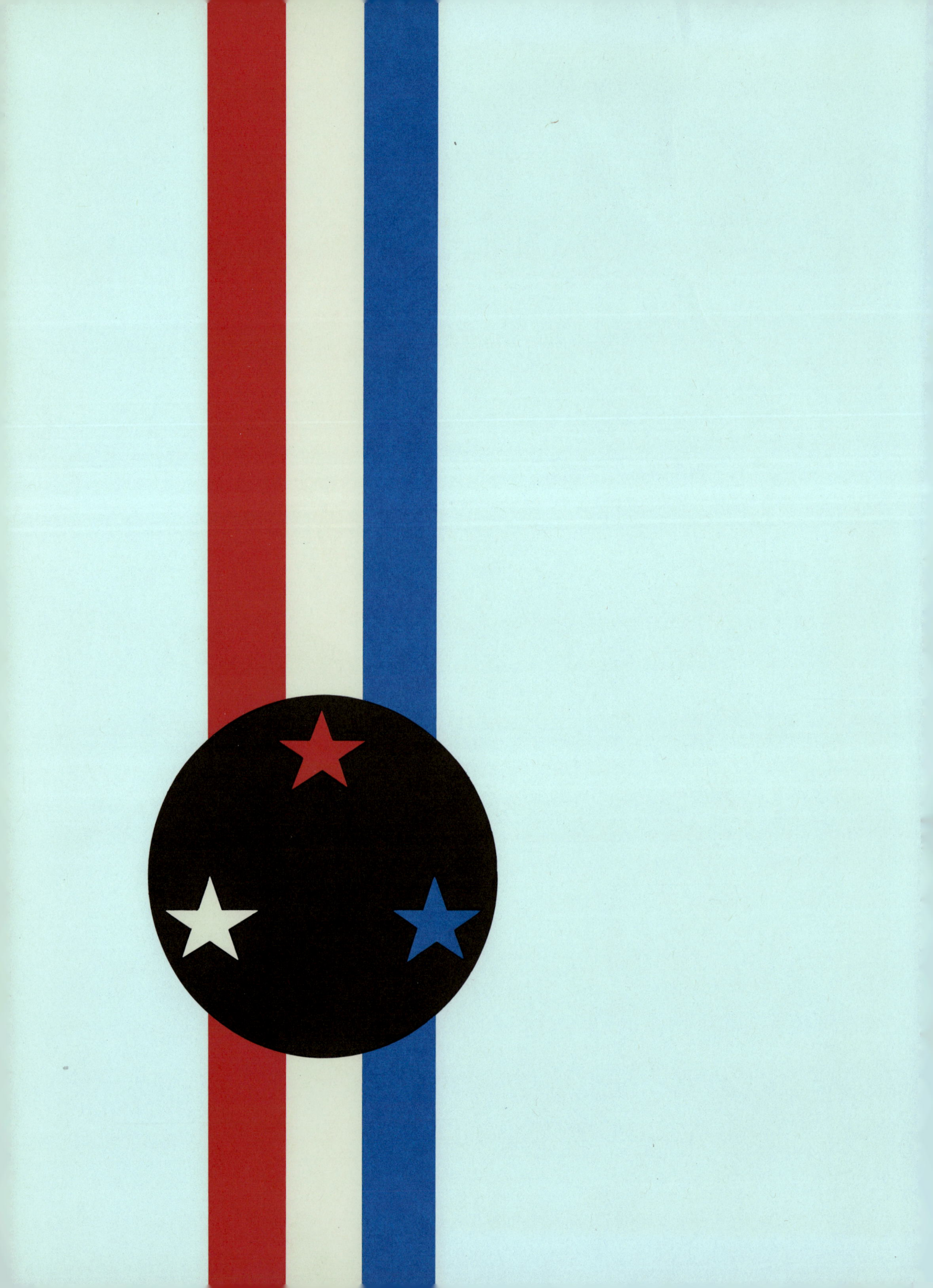